The Dark Side

Adrian Tilley

U0106712

QX PUBLISHING CO.

The Dark Side

Author: Adrian Tilley

Editor: Betty Wong

Published by:
QX PUBLISHING CO.
8/F, Eastern Central Plaza, 3 Yiu Hing Road, Shau Kei Wan, Hong Kong

Printed by:
Elegance Printing & Book Binding Co. Ltd., Block A, 4/F, Hoi Bun Industrial Building, Hong Kong

Edition:
First edition, March 2015
© 2015 QX PUBLISHING CO.

ISBN 978 962 255 115 2

Printed in Hong Kong.

The Dark Side: A Preface

To Young Readers

Welcome to 'The Dark Side'. We all like a story that chills us and thrills us. We lead safe lives and want to take our risks but do it safely through the stories we read. We can be shocked or horrified or made afraid but know that when we put the book down , everything will be normal again. Some of the stories here might make us re-think what 'normal' means. There are lots of different 'normals'. Just imagine that vampires, werewolves and zombies are 'normal'.

These stories have one thing in common: they are all about Hong Kong teens, caught in situations they can't escape from. Well, you all have that experience, don't you? Home, school, family, friends sometimes. The teens here though are trapped by other...forces, all evil. And there aren't many happy endings.

Ever wanted revenge on a teacher? Had a date that went bad? Had a friend who wasn't a friend at all? These things are here — but worse than you can ever imagine.

And it all happens here in Hong Kong — places you know, you visit, you love. Perhaps you won't see those places quite the same any more...but enjoy anyway!

To Parents and Teachers

Reading fiction is vital to the development of language skills. All the educational research proves that. Get young people reading fiction — get them hooked — and language and creativity and imagination follow.

The tradition of horror stories goes back to Charles Dickens, Edgar Allan Poe and Thomas Hardy. Long before that, such tales were told around campfires and were a part of the oral tradition of story-telling. Readers and listeners have always loved a visit to the Dark Side.

Horror stories require vivid description, real situations, believable and sympathetic characters. It's often what's NOT said, what's NOT described — just hinted at — that's the most frightening part. What we IMAGINE is where fear lies.

All but one of the central characters is female, not because they make the best 'helpless, screaming victims' in horror stories. No, here it is the female who is active, ingenious, resourceful and who sometimes gets it totally wrong.

Whether the reader is female or male, these stories should surprise and shock the reader. Some may cause an occasional smile. 'I didn't expect that to happen!' is the response I'm after. Most importantly for you, as parents and teachers, is to talk to the young readers about the stories. Share the magic, the fear, the horror with them.

Adrian Tilley

Contents

The Dream Gate

Hai-dee was late for school. She was never late so she was annoyed — with herself, with her alarm which didn't go off, with her mother who forgot to wake her, with the dog which didn't come and lick her nose that morning. It was all their fault, she kept telling herself as she half-ran, half-walked through the park, through the estate to school.

The playground was empty and no-one was on the gate for once. She scampered up the stair well, her bag banging on her back. No assembly today so straight to the form room — 42E. She stood outside the door, took a deep breath and pushed it open.

The room was very quiet. She kept her eyes on her toes and slid to her desk, sat and hauled her bag onto her lap. Within seconds she had everything laid out perfectly: pens, pencils, ruler. English exercise book opened to last night's homework. Only then did she peer up at the teacher expecting Miss Chan's eyes to be burning into hers.

But they weren't. Miss Chan wasn't watching anything. Her head was on her arms on the desk and she appeared to be…asleep. If Miss Chan was asleep then the class would be up to trouble with a capital… .

Hai-dee's eyes scanned the room. At every desk heads were bowed, resting on arms, hands, books, pencil cases, bags. But every head! Everyone was asleep.

Hai-dee took a deep breath. This was a bit annoying. Why weren't they all awake and aware that Hai-dee, for the first time in her life, had been late. This momentous event — this huge break with tradition — had gone unnoticed.

'Hello, anyone.' (quiet.)

'Hello, anyone.' (louder.)

'Hello, ANYONE!' (very loud.)

No-one stirred. Not a snuffle or a snort. Just a murmuration of deep, regular breathing.

'What's going on? Is this some sort of a joke? If it is, it isn't very funny!'

No response. Surely at some point, they were all going to jump up and shout and point at her. She waited, bracing herself for the gale of laughter. Nothing.

The girl walked over to the teacher's desk and bent in towards the slumped head with the hair pulled back in a tight pony tail.

'Miss! Miss Chan! Can you wake up? Can you wake up now? Please?'

The 'please' came out really loud and Hai-dee's hand had grabbed the teacher's shoulder. Still nothing.

This is all wrong, she told herself. All wrong. I'd better report it. Perhaps there has been a gas leak; it could be dangerous. She hurried to the door.

And that is when it hit her. The wall of silence that surrounded her, penned her in. The whole school was silent.

Something really had gone wrong. She scuttled to the next classroom — 43A. She peered through the glass window in the door. No movement. No sound. Just slumped heads in five rows. In Room 44B — the same.

Now she ran into the next corridor of rooms. But it was the same. Sleeping. Sleeping sickness — because that is what it must be. She'd heard of an African disease or something. It had struck the school. They'd all been bitten by a mosquito. No a fly. A tse-tse fly — that was it. The fly that caused the sleeping sickness. She'd read all about it in a biology book.

Maybe the office would be open. Someone would know what was going on and would be calling doctors, ambulances, police. Surely? The office looked in its usual state of organised chaos with piles of papers, boxes, registers except no-one was moving. Everyone was slumped.

'Ring home,' rattled through her brain. 'Ring the police,' clicked another proposal.

'Get the hell out of here. Now!' That thought made her knees turn to water and her heart bumped against her ribs.

She ran back to 42E, snatched up her bag and skip-jumped down the stairs. Still no-one stirred. Her hand dived into her bag and retrieved her mobile phone. She clicked it on, scrolled to 'H' and pressed for 'Home'. The phone buzzed.

'Come on, answer it.'

Buzz buzz. Buzz buzz.

The whole school was silent.

'I know you're there. Someone's there.'

And then it hit her. There was someone there probably. But like everyone at school, they were asleep too. She remembered she had run out of the flat without trying to speak to anyone because she was late and hadn't noticed that...they were probably all asleep.

She ran to the outside door and stepped out into the hot September sunshine. And there it was. The silence. The overwhelming silence of a city gone to sleep.

But if they...the rest of the world was asleep, why wasn't she? What made her different? What hadn't she done? What had she done to make her awake? When had all this happened, exactly? In the last few minutes? Why hadn't she noticed on the way to school? This was a different world totally from her usual world. Totally different. It was silent.

Hai-dee had reached the school gates and nearly waved at the security man in his hut but she stopped herself. He was asleep too, of course. Then she saw the street. Cars, buses, vans, all stopped at odd angles on the road. Everything had rolled slowly to stillness. No-one had run into anyone else or anything. They had all simply come to a standstill. Drivers were slumped like dead parachutists at their wheels. Bus windows were full of leaning heads. On the pavements, people were stretched out or coiled up or sat on their haunches.

She threaded her way through the chaos, not daring to look too closely at anyone. If they were hurt she would have to do something. As long as they just slept, she didn't want to, couldn't, do anything.

She looked up. If cars had stopped what about the planes? There were vapour trails across the blue sky. Nothing was dropping down. Nothing ploughing into skyscrapers like those planes in New York…so long ago before she was born. All the planes must be flying automatically…as normal.

The sky was clear but her head was cloudy. She was standing outside a fruit shop. A box of dragon fruit lay there — their horny red skins like swollen lizards, made her feel sick — but she reached out and held one. Behind the row of boxes, the old woman shopkeeper was sat staring at her. Hai-dee dropped the fruit and froze. Then she realised the woman was asleep. She was one of those people who slept with their eyes open. Weird.

Hai-dee's hands grabbed the fruit again, tore at the greasy red skin and peeled it back. The white, flecked flesh of the fruit was there. She sunk her teeth into its softness, gulping back the sweet chunks, not chewing them, feeling them lumpily slide down her throat into her stomach.

'Well, I had no breakfast. I'm starving,' she told herself.

She threw the fruit on the pavement hard. It sprayed out in pieces, the lump of red skin slithering into the gutter.

Hai-dee felt a scream bubble from her throat and suddenly there it was, chasing around and across the silent street.

'Help me!'

Over and over she screamed. Then stopped suddenly. It

wasn't her who needed help. It was everyone else. It was the sleepers who needed help. She couldn't do anything on her own.

Perhaps she should hide. Hide until everyone woke up. Like a hide-and-seek game. She walked fast towards the main square, stepping over and around people, dodging between cars and vans parked half way across the pavements. Always she avoided looking at the faces of the people around her. She was afraid of their sleeping but what if one of them awoke and found her alone. What might happen then? She closed her eyes to blank it out.

When she opened her eyes that was when she caught sight of a movement in the corner of her sight. Her heart throbbed and she froze mid-stride. The movement was above her but now had gone. She stepped around and the moving thing was there again.

On the huge screen fixed to the front of the store, an image of Hai-dee flickered with life and movement. A street cam was being projected onto the screen: it was mounted somewhere above her. She looked up and her image lifted its head and looked. She lifted her arm and the image waved in unison. She jumped. The image jumped. She danced wildly, flinging her arms out, hopping over, jumping over bodies on the ground, in a mad frenzy. She was shouting — stupid senseless stuff — she was twisting and swirling, everything disjointed, like a puppet dangling on the strings of a twitching, mad puppeteer. On and on she went, springing and spinning round the square, her other self mimicking her exactly ten metres above her. On and on, turning wider and wider, out of control on the edges of the square.

Hai-dee felt her brain swirling, felt the dizziness growing within her, a feeling of nausea. She wanted to be sick but she kept spinning. In a moment she would collapse in mad exhaustion and then she could join in, give in to sleep and be like the rest. Just disappear into sleep.

But it didn't happen like that. She fell forward, her hands reaching out to catch the ground as it rushed up towards her. The pavement caught her knee first, gashing it open. She rolled forward, then onto her back, clutching her leg, one hand over the knee. Now she cried out in pain. A piece of skin hung loose. Underneath it was raw red and scuffed up in an ugly triangle of pain. Tears slid down her face but she blinked the rest back, pressing at her wound with the flat of her hand. She needed a bandage.

The blue sign of the chemist shop glowed clearly — a beacon for all to see. The doors slid automatically open and Hai-dee limped into the cold, air-conditioned store. Some displays had been tumbled by sleepers. Some shelves had their contents sprawled across the floor on top of sleeping bodies. She found the medical section — the rows of plasters, ointments, creams, pills — all the things that would make people well, if only they were awake.

She took a crepe bandage roll, tore off the wrapping and began winding it round her knee. She nibbled the edge of the material and tugged off the end, splitting it then tying it, like her mother had when the children had accidents at home. The bandage was tight and already eased the pain. That was when she realised what she had at that moment.

Total freedom. She could do whatever she wanted. She slipped the bag from her shoulders and opened it up then tipped all the contents onto the floor — the few books she hadn't taken out and put on her desk at school. Then she simply filled the bag. It was easy. Make-up. Hair spray. Shampoo bottles — the expensive stuff she could never afford. She was worth it! Box after box of perfume. Her hands pushed the loot in tight, she slid the zip across and heaved it onto her shoulders. As she exited she looked up at the security camera above the door and blew it a kiss. It doesn't matter any more, does it?

And now fear had gone from inside Hai-dee. Fear had gone. To be replaced by excitement. The excitement of being able to do whatever she wanted to do. No-one would or could stop her. She swirled down the street to the row of designer shops — Versace, Balenciaga, Boss, Vuitton — she could hardly pronounce their stupid foreign names. All the shops she could never go in. She stepped over the young attendant with spiked hair and the neat, black suit.

'Thank you, young man. But I am buying today. Well, I'm not actually. I'm stealing.'

The word felt odd in her mouth. Stealing. She'd never done anything like this ever. Never, ever had she stole anything. But now she wanted to steal. And she did. She flipped rack after rack of neatly labelled coats, tops, dresses around the floor. She hooked out her samples, held them in front of her before the mirror. If she liked them they joined a pile on the floor. If she didn't like them, they flapped wildly through the air landing loosely on immaculate sleeping sales staff.

When she left, Hai-dee had her purchases stuffed in two big bags she carried in each hand like heavy buckets of water. She nodded politely to the door boy and headed off down the street.

She did arrive home eventually to a silent block as she expected. Hai-dee stopped outside the door and reality sprang at her for the first time. What would she tell her mother when she awoke which she was bound to do at some time? How would she explain the bags of designer clothes and perfumes? Could she hide them in her room? Of course she couldn't. She could sell them to get rid of them. Give some money to her mother. Her mind was racing ahead and the front door stayed closed. Of course, she had no key. She relied on her mother letting her in.

'Mother! Mother! Wake up! Let me in! Let me in!' she shouted up at the windows.

Soon she was kicking the door then looking for something to smash it with. A metal bar from the back of a builder's van would do. Hai-dee swung hard and heard the wood splinter.

THIS WAS AN EMERGENCY. HE NEEDED TO ACT.

Constable Jung Chun peered down at the block below. The sound of splintering wood drew his attention to a figure at the door of the low rise flats across the street. Whatever else was happening — and he didn't understand this sleeping sickness panic, what it was or why it was happening — what this person was doing was very wrong. Against the law. The person was looting — just look at all those bags. Now they were trying to burgle the house. This was an emergency situation. He needed to act. His hand reached to the leather pouch on his waist and eased out the shiny black service pistol.

Hai-dee had decided as she reached through the hole in the door to unlock it, she would get her mother to agree to selling 'the loot' and share the gains. Or more probably her mother would make her take it all back and apologise. Still, she'd enjoyed her little bit of freedom hadn't she? It had been fun.

She was puzzled by the thump on the side of her head. The fine drizzle of blood that sprayed across the door and her hands. Puzzled by the excruciating pain in her ear, her teeth coming loose, her jaw moving strangely sideways. And then what was this darkness that was dropping in on her? Like sudden sleep?

The Pop-up

Mister Wong had a big, flat nose and he talked through it. Well, snuffled through it — like a pig with its nose in a trough. It was a flippy, floppy sound and it was the same whether he was angry or happy or anything. Schnurrflurrppp.

Mei Ling hated it when he stood or worse, crouched behind her to check what she was doing on the screen. She imagined he was going to schnurrful stuff all over her shoulder or all over her hair. She was very nervous when he was close.

'Well, Mei Ling, (schnurrrfff) have you managed to log on? (flurrrpp)'

Mei-Ling (not looking round, just staring at the screen): 'Yes, Mr Wong.'

'Good (schnurr). And you know what to do then?'

Mei Ling: 'Yes, Mr Wong, schhrrr.'

'What?'

'Yes, Mr Wong, sir.'

Mei Ling heard a giggle behind her. All the kids loathed Mr Wong and his snuffle. He was disgusting. They all agreed. They would all have liked him to be removed. That Miss Chang was a much nicer teacher. She smiled. She didn't give you much homework. She didn't turn up on time so lessons were short. And she didn't snuffle. Yes, thought Mei Ling, better Mr Wong just went.

She hammered in her password. The screen flickered and the school page came up. All the usual boring stuff. All those kids looking happy as if they were having the times of their lives. Mei Ling looked around the room. Was anyone smiling? No. Was anyone having the time of their life? No. And all because Mister Wong snuffled. Get rid of Mister Wong. Get rid of the snuffle. Happiness. Everyone smiles.

A pop-up glooped into the side bar on the left. A pop-up? That was unusual. The web security system stopped them.

'Your chance to change your life! Genie.com.'

Mei Ling glanced over her shoulder. No-one watching. She clicked onto the site. A little cartoon face in one of those funny red Arabian hats beamed at her. The genie — of course. The man who makes magic happen.

'Lucky you! This is your lucky day!'

Mei Ling grinned. Oh yes, of course it is. That's why I'm in this awful Technology lesson with the Big Snuffle.

A big number 3 jumped onto the screen, flashing bright red.

'You have 3 wishes. And the Genie will guarantee those three wishes will be granted.'

She had to stop herself chuckling out loud. The Snuffle would hear her and then it would be trouble — using an illegal web-site on school equipment. She leaned in so her face and shoulders shielded the screen.

'Just type in your three wishes below. Press enter. And you are a winner. You don't have to use all your wishes immediately. But they must be used within one week from now. Good luck! Happy wishing and enjoy!'

The genie boy smiled a big white smile and his hands pointed down the page to the three numbered boxes. Mei Ling's mind went blank. *Any* wish? Any wish at all? Oh my God. So many things to wish for. She liked Kevin Chan in the group. She liked him a lot. She wanted him to like her but she knew he wasn't interested. Perhaps the Genie could fix it. Her fingers clicked across the keyboard,

'A date with Kevin Chan.'

She closed her eyes and for a few moments imagined how happy she would be if it happened. Kevin Chan as her bf. A smile hung on her face.

The piece of paper landed in her lap. It had been loosely rolled up and flicked her way from somewhere in the class. She was about to complain when she saw Kevin Chan grinning at her. Her heart jumped in her chest. Kevin was grinning at her. He was nodding too, nodding at the piece of paper in her hand. She felt stupid — of course he wanted her to look at it. He'd flicked it at her. Kevin Chan had flicked paper at her. Her day was getting better every second that passed.

Her fingers were clumsy pressing the paper flat. There were words on the paper. He'd written it upside down. No, she was holding the paper the wrong way round. She looked at his face. His gorgeous, smiling face with that floppy fringe. Kevin Chan — whose hands had written these words for her.

'Want to go to the cinema tonight? Nod three times if yes.'

Why is everything in threes today? Thought Mei Ling. One nod would have been enough. She nodded three times and looked at him again. He was smiling broadly and nodded back three times.

'Mei Ling, schnurrrff...don't you have anything to do schnurrfllle...except stare at Kevin Chan?'

The class let out a big 'Oooooooh.' Mei Ling's head snapped to the front. She didn't want Mr Wong seeing the Genie. The round cartoon face was grinning at her. She swallowed hard. The magic worked. The Genie worked. She'd asked for a date with dear, delightful Kevin Chan and the Genie had provided.

'Thank you, Genie,' she mouthed.

She put a kiss on her fingers and pressed it on his face on the screen.

'You have two wishes left.'

The words flashed. Thoughts hopped and ran and jumped through Mei Ling's mind. If the Genie could fix Kevin Chan, perhaps it would work with Mr Wong. And before she could stop herself she typed in the words:

Get rid of Mister Wong.

Her finger jolted on 'enter'. Would it be so quick again? Would the Genie work again? Would Mr Wong just evaporate?

'Mei Ling, schlurrrff. Why are you sitting with your fingers crossed? You can't type like that. Get on with your work.'

Obviously no magic after all. There was no real Genie. No magic. The note from Kevin was just coincidence. She popped the red cross in the corner of the pop-up, ignoring the flashing words.

'You have one more wish.'

All a silly game. She had better things to do. Like think of Kevin Chan. She squeezed the paper in her hands remembering how Kevin had written on the paper. To her. School was so much more…satisfying. And Mr Wong's snuffles didn't really matter any more.

Mei Ling was still smiling the next day when she walked into school. Her feet seemed to be hovering above the pavement. Her head felt light. The cinema had been good fun. They'd laughed a lot. Spilled a lot of pop corn. And a miserable gweilo just behind told Kevin off for using his mobile phone in the dark. At the end of the evening Kevin had said he would like to see her again. She nodded — three times — and they laughed a lot again.

'No form base lessons today. Go straight to the playground for assembly.'

The tinny words of the school announcement cut through Mei Ling's thoughts and she automatically followed the clumps of students now changing direction for assembly. The playground quickly filled up with lines of students, all looking round, shuffling their feet, unsure of what was going on.

We only have special assemblies when something has gone wrong, thought Mei Ling. Or very right. Perhaps we're all here to celebrate my date with Kevin Chan. She looked along the line knowing she couldn't just go and stand by him. He was there but he hadn't seen her. She liked that — watching him and him not knowing.

'Quiet in line,' hissed the form teacher, Miss Ling. Mei Ling noticed the woman's face was tight. Her eyes were watery and looked a bit swollen.

'What's going on, Miss Ling?' she asked as her teacher passed down the line.

'You'll find out. Be patient. Quiet in line!'

Miss Ling was stressed out — that was for sure.

Then the Principal appeared on the platform. The microphone whistled in complaint as she got too close. She tapped it irritably and looked across at one of the technicians.

'Is this ok?'

The technician nodded. Only once. They weren't dating then.

The Principal pulled herself up straight. Her shoulders had been sagging with some unseen weight till then. She was tall and her dark blue suit made her taller, bigger — more imposing. Mei Ling had the growing sense that something very important was about to happen.

'Students and staff — school. I've called this special

assembly because I have some bad news, some very bad news to tell you.'

The ranks of students all seemed to shudder, as if bracing themselves. Mei Ling's mind raced. Had there been a fire? Had some students done something really bad? Was the school going to close down?

'Yesterday evening, Mr Wong, our IT teacher, was involved in an accident in Victoria Harbour.'

Mei Ling imagined him splurrrffffing in the water. Students were looking at each other with small, wicked smiles.

'Sadly, Mr Wong died. He drowned. It was a matter of very bad luck. He missed his footing on the ferry and fell. He was crushed by the boat.'

Mei Ling's heart actually stopped beating. And her breathing stopped. And her brain went numb. Just for a moment everything went blank. Wong was dead. The snuffler was gone. He'd died a terrible, painful death. An awful way to die. Hideously painful. Horribly painful.

Mei Ling closed her eyes tightly. She was afraid that when she opened them the whole school would be looking at her and pointing their fingers.

'Mei Ling killed him! Mei Ling killed him!'

She opened her eyes. No. Everyone was facing forward, staring glumly at the Principal.

'Mr Wong has been here many years and we're all sad to lose him in such…tragic circumstances.'

The Principal's voice had a catch in it. She was on the

edge of crying.

'For lesson one you will be with your form teacher to talk about what has happened with Mr Wong. If any of you want to talk to me, that's fine. It is a very sad day for the school.'

The Principal turned and her heels clicked off the platform. Mei Ling's eyes were fixed on her own feet. The blood was pounding in her head. She wanted to be sick, right there, in front of everyone, all over her shiny school shoes. Her brain seemed to be exploding in her head.

I have killed Mr Wong. I have killed Mr Wong. I made that wish and now he's dead. And now he's…dead.

She saw him falling: the splash, the dull clunk as the ferry swung onto the pier, his cry, the pain, the blood in the water. Then she was sick. Everyone shouted and jumped away. Then she fainted.

Miss Ling, the form teachers, seemed to be floating above her, talking to her, smiling.

'You're going to be ok, Mei Ling. You're fine.'

Mei Ling knew she wasn't going to be fine. She'd killed someone. She was a murderer.

'It was perhaps the shock at hearing the news about Mr Wong. You liked him a lot, I suppose.'

No, I didn't, thought Mei Ling. I didn't like him a lot. In fact I hated him. Loathed him. I couldn't stand him being near me. But that's no reason to kill anyone.

Miss Ling's hand felt her forehead.

'You're a bit too warm. Better just sit here for a bit and recover I'll come and see you in a little while.'

A blue plastic chair had appeared and Mei Ling perched on it. She realised she wasn't in the playground any more but in the medical room. It smelled of disinfectant. That smell made her feel ill straightaway.

Now she was alone and all the thoughts came crowding in. Why had she done it? What was the Genie thing? What if other people had used it? All sorts of bad things might happen. She had to warn people. But then everyone would know what she had done. She had killed Mr Wong. She couldn't tell anyone. She daren't. She couldn't trust anyone, could she?

The door rattled and Kevin Chan's smiling face appeared. Oh no! Kevin. She wanted to see him but he was the last person she wanted to see. Could she tell him? Could she trust him? He would hate her for what she did. He would never have done what she did.

'Hello, Mei Ling. You feeling any better? You don't look so good.'

'I'll be fine, I think. Just a bit shaken up, you know?'

He sat on the bed and looked into her eyes.

'It just shows you care so much about people.'

No! She wanted to scream. I murdered him! I'm a horrible person!

'I don't know what came over me. I don't know what made me do it. I wasn't thinking straight.'

'You were just a bit overcome. That's all.'

'It was stupid. The stuff came up and bang! I responded.'

'We get sick pretty quickly. It can't be helped.'

'I'm not talking about sick. About being sick. I'm talking about…'

She swallowed the words.

'You're not making sense, Mei Ling. It's the reaction. Poor guy. What a way to go. Crushed to death.'

'Shut up, Kevin! Shut up! I know how he died. I know. I know why he died.'

'None of us can know that. It was an accident. Bad karma.'

Mei Ling's hands grasped Kevin's arm.

'But it wasn't an accident, Kevin. It wasn't. He was killed.'

Kevin pulled away, embarrassed. He stood up and looked towards the door.

'Mei Ling, you're pretty confused right now. Maybe you better try to sleep. I'll get Miss Ling to come and see you again.'

And before she could tell him about the pop-up, Genie. com and the three wishes, he had gone. He wouldn't have believed her anyway. And nor would Miss Ling. No, she had to live with this secret for the rest of her life.

It was six days later — six days of feeling sick, trembling, being unable to concentrate on anything. Six days of 'Are you alright, Mei Ling?' 'Is something wrong?' 'Do you want the sick bay?' Six days of Kevin avoiding her because she was embarrassing. Six days of having her head filled with the battered and bloody body of Mister Wong, his flesh eaten by fish, his broken bones sticking out through blue-white skin… six days and here she was again in the computer room, sat in front of the same computer. Miss Chang was taking the lesson and there was no snuffling. No Mister Wong.

'Hello again, lucky you! This is your lucky day!'

Mei Ling jumped back from the screen. The pop-up was there. The round Genie face smiling at her. She put her hand over the face but could still see the flashing words.

'You still have one more wish. Don't waste it.'

She thought she could wish herself dead but then the idea came to her. She could put it all right. She could change things back with Genie.com. Of course! Reverse the magic. If it works one way it will work the other. Her fingers rattled the keyboard.

'Bring back Mr Wong as our teacher.'

Then she slumped on her chair. The pop-up popped down with a final message.

'Thank you. Good luck! And goodbye!'

Mei Ling sat in a silent daze while the class buzzed around her. What a stupid idea, expecting Mr Wong to come back. Stupid.

She was sitting by the door and heard the footsteps quite clearly — slow and shuffling like something was being dragged along. Then there was a shape at the door — she could see it through the opaque glass. It was a person but they didn't seem to standing up properly, just slumped to one side. Was that water seeping under the door? And the sudden smell of sea water? You couldn't mistake that. The door handle turned and Mei Ling dived forward to stop the door opening but she was too late. She knew who...what it was but it was too late.

That was when the screaming began and went on and on and on.

School of the Walking Dead

Hi. I'm Rosie. I'm in what they call the Undead Class. UD for short. It's a stupid name really because we are all dead and have been for some time but because of some freak of nature, I guess, we're all still alive and kicking. Well, in my case, alive but I don't do much kicking. I'm not into sport and that stuff. In the school prospectus it says we're the Forever Class which sounds nice but means we never get to leave. We stay exactly as we are. Forever. I'm fifteen and I'm going to be in the Forever Class, well, forever. But it's fun — we all get along with each other pretty well. When you're going to be with someone for eternity, it's probably a good thing.

There are other classes in school. The Lupus Class is for werewolves. Lupus is some fancy name for wolf. Healthy is in Lupus — he's the guy I'm dating. He's cute really — quite normal, with these big, brown eyes and a wide smile. And it's fine he's a werewolf until every once in a while there's a full moon. He doesn't like talking about it. He's shy like that.

'Tell me what happens, Healthy,' I'll say.

'It's just not so nice. I don't like it,' he'll say. 'The hair. And the teeth. And going on all fours. It's just…horrible. You wouldn't like me.'

I smile and tell him, 'I used to have a pet dog when I was alive. I like dogs.'

" The hair. And the teeth. And going on all fours. It's just...horrible."

But he shakes his head. 'You wouldn't like me.'

So we don't talk about it much. But I'm curious. Not many girls can say their bf can change into a mad wolf once in a while. Though some boys are like mad wolves anyway, all the time.

There's Vampire Class too but it's a night class so we don't get to see them during the day. The kids there keep pretty busy. There's always some TV company coming to sign them up for yet another vampire show.

Then there's the Ghoul School. That's the Zombie Class but they're awful. So loud and noisy and always chasing around their block. And always eating. They're not so good looking either — you know, bits missing. Their block is very untidy, full of litter everywhere. Eyes, hands, sometimes arms. They have a big lost property office. But it's okay because they're locked up all the time. At lunchtimes Healthy and I go down to the block just to listen. It's fun. The howling and the screaming and battering on the doors to be let out. Makes us feel better about ourselves.

The school is pretty big — like a village and we all live there all the time. We're not allowed to go out to meet Normals. They say it's too dangerous. Normals generally don't like us. They think we're weird and abnormal, which to them, we are. Healthy and I talk about Normals a lot and I like reading these silly romantic stories where young Normals meet and fall in love and then life gets messy for them. Silly stuff I guess, but lots of UD girls read it.

Normal Land. It's out there and once we went for it.

'We could sneak out. Skip class and just go walk around for a bit. See what they're like,' Healthy said.

'But how do we get through security? There's an electric fence and guards.'

Healthy smiled a twinkly smile that made his teeth look like a toothpaste advert.

'When I was…er, in wolf mode…I dug a tunnel with my claws.'

He looked down at his fingers. He keeps his nails really nice.

'We could use the tunnel. I keep it hidden.'

I wanted to ask more but I could see he was a bit embarrassed. So there we were, crawling through a wolf tunnel to Normal Land. I followed him on all fours — he seemed to move so much more quickly and easier than me but I didn't say anything. He'd have been hurt.

Normal Land — it was my first visit since becoming UD — was, well, normal. Once we got into the town, it seemed very busy. Everyone scurrying round, shopping, queuing for buses, old men on cell phones shouting at the top of their voices (perhaps the phones weren't switched on so they had to shout). Everything seemed…normal. They didn't seem to notice a pale (very pale — deathly pale I suppose) girl with lots of eye makeup (I thought it improved my eyes) in rather worn out clothes that were a bit out of date. But then I did see quite a few girls like me and they were definitely not UD.

And no-one noticed Healthy either because he looked healthy. A good diet I suppose.

'You know what will happen if they find out I'm a werewolf, don't you?' said Healthy as we wandered through a wet market where lots of raw meat was hanging up. Perhaps it was the meat that set him thinking this way.

'Erm…actually, Healthy, I don't. Remember, this is my first time in Normal Land. You've been here lots of times.'

Then I saw his face drop. He didn't want reminding of that, obviously.

'That doesn't count. I'm in wolf mode then.' He forced himself to be brighter.' Anyway, they'll all try to kill. Guys will run out with guns and silver bullets.'

'Do they have those things? I thought that was just in stories.'

Healthy shook his head sadly.

'All the chemists stock silver bullets. Since werewolves got official recognition as a minority group. Court of Human Rights and all that. So it's pretty…dangerous. Like hunting season all year round.'

I gave him a little hug.

'We'll be careful, Healthy. Let's get a coffee somewhere.'

He took me to a place called Pacific Coffee or something where Normals sit at tables and stare at their cell phones instead of talking to each other. Healthy looked carefully around.

'Sometimes you can spot some of our lot who've skipped

out of school.'

I stared around at what I thought were Normals.

'You mean some of these could be…?'

I stared more carefully trying to spot something different, something mortal.

'There's a guy over there who's very hairy.'

Healthy shook his head. 'No, he's just hairy.'

And that's when things went very badly wrong. I'd noticed this guy at the internet desk in a long, black coat trying to look like he wasn't there. There was something familiar about the way he was crouched over, typing with one hand. Then I saw his sleeve was empty. I stared at it and he saw me staring out of the corner of his eye, an eye that was kind of lolling sideways a bit.

I grabbed Healthy's arm. 'Don't look now, Healthy, but that's a zombie on the internet.'

Whenever you say 'Don't look now' people always do, crane their necks and stare around. Healthy did. And that's when the zombie exploded. Not literally. He jumped up, made a roaring noise with his mouth wide open and pointed at us. I have to say his teeth weren't in good shape — perhaps all that tearing at raw flesh. But it wasn't pretty, that mouth.

Everyone in the coffee place was on their feet. Chairs were knocked over. Drinks spilled. The floor looked like a massive cappuccino coffee. Healthy grabbed my arm and pulled me up and away as old zombie-features lurched towards us. We couldn't reason with him that we, too, were not Normals and he would be better to pursue…other flesh. There just wasn't time and he didn't look in any mood to reason about anything. His eyes were too blood-shot to see logic and he looked angry. And hungry. Not a good combination when it comes to reasoned debate, I've found.

We were through the door, bumping and bouncing off Normals who were screaming very loudly indeed. Zombie-head had skidded on the cappuccino floor and fell against a table, quite hard, with his head. An ear flipped through the air — a bit a like a custard tart — and landed on the counter where the girl serving couldn't get out. Zombie-head got up and shuffled towards her, feeling where his ear had been. She had nowhere to go and was crying quite hard as he got close. In desperation, I think, she took the ear, placed it on a plate and held it out to him. She might have been hoping for a tip, I guess. But he just ripped her throat out. So ungrateful, these ghouls. They certainly don't teach them manners in Ghoul School. He had no manners at all.

Healthy and I just kept running along with everyone else. Two hard-faced men in uniforms were running the other way pulling out black pistols as they moved.

'Get down and stay down!' they shouted and everyone seemed to obey, cowering on the ground with their arms over their heads.

I suppose if you're a UD or a werewolf you don't think so

' But he just ripped her throat out.
So ungrateful, those ghouls.'

much about losing your life. For us it doesn't work that way. I wanted to just get out of there but Healthy pulled me down and signalled for me to copy everyone else.

We could hear the zombie shouting and making a scene at the other end of the mall. But where we were, everyone was looking at a young teen boy with his hood up still running.

'Non-normal!' someone shouted from nearby.

'Non-normal!' a lot of people joined in, pointing at him.

I recognised him. He was UD in the class above. An A student. Hardworking. Happy. What was he doing here? Why didn't he get down like everyone else? Then I saw where he was running. Or who he was running to. A pretty girl in jeans and a t-shirt was waving at him from the entrance to a clothes shop. Was she waving or signalling for him to get down? She was definitely a Normal and she was smiling to see him but worried because she wanted him to get down on the ground.

I could only guess what their story was but they looked like they wanted to be in each other's arms. That's when the bullet took him in the back of his head.

Healthy said later it was one hell of a shot from that distance. The security guy had just turned and in one movement took aim and let off one shot.

The boy crumpled and fell to the floor. His head was a mess. Some people were screaming. The girl in the shop ran forward and she was really shouting and crying. As she got to the body, that's when things went badly wrong again. Him being a UD, well he started to get up but he was a mess. Some of his head was missing and there was nasty stuff on his shoulders and on the floor. He reached out to her and that's when she began screaming. Screaming really loud.

She obviously had no idea he was a UD. Not until that moment when he stood up and looked at her with half his face. He looked kind of hurt and puzzled at her reaction. Healthy covered my eyes and pulled me away and on our hands and knees we crawled out of the mall. As we reached the exit there were more gunshots from the other end of the mall. The zombie's shouting stopped. There was silence. Then a whole lot more screaming.

To be honest, we were glad when we were back in that tunnel again.

'I don't think I want to go to Normal Land again,' I said. 'It's so...freaky.'

Healthy just nodded wisely.

So there you are. Healthy and I still hang out together in school and we're happy. Maybe we'll be happy together forever like the songs say. Just sometimes he seems a little weird and he says sorry and I don't see him for a day or two. But other than that, I guess we're pretty, well...normal. Like any teenagers.

Mrs. Wicca — The Witch of Lantau

October 31st 1965

A dark night. A very dark night for Halloween in that little town nestling by the sea…not unlike this one. And in the murky streets, where normally there would have been silence at this time of day, children were playing.

Children were playing noisily — running and shouting and laughing and squealing and skipping and jumping in and out of the rows of houses. For this was Halloween — when anyone and everyone could celebrate — just for one night — the supernatural and…evil.

Pumpkin heads flickered in doorways. Parents peeped through curtains to check…just in case. But of course their children were safe. Of course they were. Halloween was for children…to play.

But for one group the fun of Trick or Treat had worn off. They had pockets full of sweets. They'd had more cake than they could eat. Their fingers were sticky with chocolate dropped on the floor. Their masks were getting loose and their costumes were tangled and smudged. The gang crumpled together under the arc of orange light from a street lamp.

Lily was the tallest and eldest — she was fourteen and knew naughty things about what adults did when they went to bed, could smoke a cigarette without going green and puking and knew lots more but wouldn't tell the others. She changed the game.

'Let's go cherry knocking. We hide near a house and one of us — I choose who — goes up to the front door, rings the bell and runs away and hides. Okay? Got it?'

The others got it. It sounded like fun.

They had got to a street that they didn't ever play in — Dante Street. It had a few houses only on one side. On the other were some trees and beyond them, the dark beach and the dark sea.

The first house had not had a small garden and a wall. The gang of five slithered into place. Lily chose Brian whose mask had been made from a cornflakes packet.

'I'll only go if Ryan comes with me,' whispered Brian, his brow crinkled. Lily shrugged her shoulders.

'Okay. Brian and Ryan first. Well? What are you waiting for?'

'I was waiting for Ryan,' said Brian.

'I was waiting for Brian,' said Ryan.

Lily hissed at them. 'Get going, stupids. You know what to do?'

'Yes,' said Brian and Ryan together and they stepped

beyond the wall, up the short path and pressed the door bell.

Ping! Ping!

A light went on in the hallway by which time Brian and Ryan were behind the wall again. The door clunked open and a woman poked her head out.

'Oh, I could have sworn the door bell went.'

She looked both ways turning her head like a puzzled chicken and closed the door.

Brian and Ryan snuffled snot into their sleeves trying to stop laughing.

'Disgusting boys,' snorted Lily and moved away.

Number 2. The house was like a reflection of Number 1 but painted green instead of grey. There was a light on upstairs.

'Celia. Your turn,' demanded Lily.

Celia, wearing red horns, poked Delia, wearing a halo she'd worn in the Nativity play at Christmas.

'Bet you daren't come with me, Delia.'

'Bet I dare,' answered Delia with a catch in her voice.

The two tip-toed to the front door but neither pressed the bell.

'Bet you daren't do it, Delia,' sneered Celia.

'Bet I dare,' sneered Delia back but before she could prove it, Celia had stabbed her finger on the glowing button, had pushed Delia against the door and run back to the cover of the wall. When Delia scrambled alongside she gave her partner a deadly look.

They could hear a thundering noise inside the house as if someone had thrown an oil drum down the stairs. The door swung open and a man stood, open mouthed, first smiling then gaping. His shirt was hanging out like a white flag.

'Doreen, so nice to see...'

His words tailed away when he realised there was no-one there. He took a step back, a step forward then back again — like a little dance of greeting or farewell — then slowly shut the door muttering something about 'kids'.

Celia and Delia just glared at one another.

Lily stood up and marched them further down the street. Number 3 was empty — no lights, no sign of life. The gang shuffled on.

There was only one house left. It was a hundred metres further on with no road or path near. Its front was like a mournful face : two dark window eyes upstairs staring out. A canopy over the front door like a broken nose and the battered and fading front door like a toothless hole where the mouth might be.

Between the gang and the house was just a stretch of muddy, beaten down grass, shining like a snail trail, leading to the door. Number 4.

'Well, I'm not going,' said Delia turning her back on the rest and looking out to sea. 'Number 4 is unlucky. It means death.'

MRS. WICCA

Ryan's head seemed to disappear into his shoulders. 'Well, I'm not going. Mrs. Wicca lives there and she's evil. Everyone knows she's a...witch. Not going.'

Lily sniffed and drew herself to her full height and looked down at the others huddled around her.

'You're pathetic. Pathetic. 'It's bad luck!' 'She's a witch!' What rubbish!'

'Well, you go, Lily, if you're so brave,' the others chorused, nodding common defiance at her.

Lily stepped away from them, her lip curled in contempt.

'Oh pathetic ones. Just watch and learn.'

And she moved off the path into the darkness towards the house at Number 4. Was there a hesitation in her step halfway there or did her foot slide on the wet grass? Did she swallow hard to get rid of that lump in the back of her throat? Did she have her lips pressed together just a little too tightly? Of course not. Not Lily.

In one of the windows, light flickered — there were candles burning inside. The old woman was too mean to use electricity like civilised people. Everyone knew Mrs. Wicca was weird. She never spoke to anyone when she passed by. She watched the children playing in the street, watched them, staring with her black eyes. Mrs. Wicca was a weirdo and deserved more than just cherry knocking. She deserved punishment…for being old and being Mrs. Wicca.

Lily's foot crashed against the front door. She turned and grinned at the others as they scuttled for cover. But Lily didn't run. Her foot lashed out again. The door rattled on its hinges.

A thin, reedy voice squeaked from inside. 'Hello! Who is it?'

Lily hammered on the door with her fist.

'Who's there?' the voice was nearer. 'What do you want?'

Lily's clenched fist pounded against the door. Her face shone with excitement.

'Who's there? Please tell me. I can't open the door until…'

Her piping words were lost to the next battering delivered by Lily.

The girl could hear the woman's shufflings behind the door, could hear her moving from one room to another, trying to move away from the thunder at her door.

'Lily!' floated Celia's voice. 'That's enough! Come back. We'll go on somewhere else.'

But the fire of hate burned in Lily's heart. She had a victim — so much more interesting than just bullying those stupid kids. She looked around the rough grass and weeds at her feet and saw what she wanted: a large, grey, shining pebble that quickly filled her hand and weighed heavy on her arm. She took two steps back, looked up at the darkened upstairs window, pulled her arm back and launched the rock.

It caught the window with a mighty smashing sound, glass spraying and tinkling in all directions. The old woman inside let out a wail like a trapped animal.

'Lily! No more!' Celia's voice was coated with panic.

The words merely drove Lily on. Something else — was it the spirit of Halloween? — had taken over. On Halloween it was right and proper to punish the witch. It was what Halloween was all about. Punishment.

A second stone was in her hand. Her eyes glinted with pleasure. And a moment later, the rock was arcing towards the window square, flickering with candlelight. She had thrown harder this time, more accurately and the whole window seemed to collapse inside. The candles flickered to almost darkness.

The scream that rang through the night air was not just fear but pain as well. She's gone back into the room. Had perhaps caught the rock in her face or perhaps the glass splinters had shredded her cheeks, her lips, her eyes.

A howl of victory came from deep inside Lily and she raised both arms above in a salute to the devastation she had wreaked on the old woman and the house. Her face was locked into a grin that bared her gums and narrowed her eyes and pulled her cheeks back till she looked like a gargoyle on a church roof.

Lily suddenly realised the others were there with her. They'd crept forward, fascinated by the energy and force coming from their leader. They stared up at her and then at the house. But no words passed.

'What are you waiting for?'

Lily's words launched them into action. They moved as one, picking up stones, sticks and clods of earth and threw them at the house, through the windows, at the door, squealing with laughter, chanting in their high voices, 'Mrs. Wicca. Mrs. Wicca. Feeling sicker. Feeling sicker.'

And Lily waved them on, signalling each throw with a flip of her hand, like a general ordering the next salvo of gunfire. The stones rattled and crashed, the lumps of earth thumped, the pieces of wood clattered. On and on they went till they could throw and howl no more, and slumped, resting their hands on the knees, sucking in air, grinning at each other, demented like some medieval vision of hell.

The moon dodged out from behind scudding cloud and sprayed silver light down on the figures in front of the house, throwing long shadows against the wall.

Inside the house was silence. A little weak yellow light fluttered at the casement of the upstairs room but movement was there none. But there was something about that light that drew Lily on. She wanted to see. She wanted to see it. What she had brought about. It.

Her hand grasped the door handle, turned and pushed.

Not locked — the old woman was too trusting. Lily stepped through into the house. There was the smell of old people: mothballs, urine, dust. This was the little living room, cluttered with little objects — sad little objects that tallied the old woman's life: jars, pots, corn dollies.

On the wall was an upside down cross, caught in the moonlight leaking through the door.

Lily walked on, the others shuffling behind her, gaping emptily at the room as they passed through. Now Lily was at the foot of the stairs looking up, as she slowly climbed, eyes fixed ahead. At the top of the stairs she could see, in the thin yellow light wavering through the half-open bedroom door, another ornament on the wall: two triangles locked together in perfect symmetry. How perfectly pretty! She reached up and sent it crashing to the floor.

On she went, drawing the others behind her into the narrow gap of the stair well. It was one step from the top that Lily paused. Something was different. Something had changed. the yellowness had gone out of the light ahead ; it had now been bleached white and was growing stronger, brighter by the moment. Could this be the moonbeams flooding in through the bedroom window? But this was not like any light Lily had seen before. It shimmered and seemed to flow into and down the stair well.

She lifted herself up the final step and now there was more

than light. There was a sound — more than a whispering, a sound like…she stepped again. There was a human voice — singing, quietly singing. How could this be? She'd heard the scream. She expected, when she turned into the bedroom to see the old woman, blood, vileness… the thought of it excited her. But now this voice, this quiet, quiet singing was bringing calm to her. Drawing her on. Drawing her up, forward, into the bedroom.

Lily gently pushed the bedroom door wide and the light flooded around her, washing across her face, her arms, her hands dirtied with nastiness, her legs.

There in front of her — in the middle of the bedroom — not the stretched out, broken corpse she'd expected — but a child, a girl of perhaps nine or ten, kneeling with her back to the door, the only movement her shoulders rising and falling with the breathing of the song. A tangle of blonde curls fell to her shoulders to brush the white silk dress that clung to her. The dress fitted tightly to her body then spread full, like a white flower, in petals around her legs.

Lily stood, locked in the doorway, as the others jostled in behind her, their eyes shining wide like saucers at the sight of the girl. Lily could not understand the words of the song — some foreign tongue that clicked the sounds and wafted the words and phrases gently into the air.

Behind her, Lily heard Brian stumble forward. The noise

made the girl turn. Lily's mouth dropped open. The child was beautiful — more beautiful than any she had ever seen: wide, blue eyes that seemed to take everything in before her, a delicate nose, a full, rosebud mouth that spoke, spoke so sweetly.

'Hello. I've been expecting you.'

Lily shook her head as if to clear it.

'Where is she? Where is Mrs Wicca?'

Lily's eyes cast around the room. There was only the girl, now smiling.

'She's gone. Mrs. Wicca's gone. You…despatched her.'

The blue eyes narrowed as if to say 'It was us, Lily. We did it. Together.'

'But where did she…?'

The question hovered and died in the air as the girl put her finger across her lips.

'Time to play!'

It was a declaration, a statement, an order, a promise. In one smooth movement the girl was on her feet and moving towards them through the white light.

'Time to play!'

And she touched Lily as she passed and that touch made Lily flinch with its coldness: when she looked down she could see a livid, red weal where the fingers had brushed her arm. She was pulled on behind the girl who parted the ring of gaping faces with her whiteness, the girl now skipping lightly down the stairs, into the sour living room, through the door smeared with mud, into the night waiting outside.

Lily and the four others moved silently behind the girl, their eyes fixed on the blonde curls in front, their mouths smiling back when the girl turned and looked over her shoulder at them, their voices joining her sweet, sweet voice.

'Girls and boys come out to play
The moon doth shine as bright as day
Lose your supper and lose your sleep
Come to your playfellows in the street.'

Now the children — for that is what they were again — were skipping in time to the gentle pulse of the song, skipping down the snail-trail path, skipping through the line of trees, skipping onto the sand of the beach glowing — was it from the moon or the light that seemed to emanate from the girl?

On and on they skipped to the water's edge where wavelets ran and slapped against wet sand and, never stopping to heed the water that splashed about their ankles and then their knees, they pushed on. The girl's dress turned dark with the water that saturated its fine fibres and it now hung heavy about her, holding her into the water.

Still the song flew from their mouths as the waves covered their waists, their chests.

'Boys and girls come out to play,
The moon doth shine as bright as day... .'

Lily watched as the water took the girl's curls and straightened them into ugly rats' tails and the girl's words were now gulps as sea water slopped across her face.

'Lose your sup...per and...looo...yu...slee'

On the girl pushed, not trying to swim or float or fight the tide but welcoming its watery embrace with smiles. And all the children smiled too and sang as the sand dipped from below their feet and the water snatched hungrily at their throats and noses. The singing died and the water clogged silence into their ears. And a darkness began to fall inside them as their breath gasped from them and the sea water plunged into them.

And as that darkness fell, Lily saw the girl beneath the water turn to smile once more but it was not the beautiful face of the child but the face of an old woman, a crone, bruised and swollen with a caved-in eye socket that stared blindly out. From a deep gash on her wrinkled forehead blood billowed endlessly in dark clouds into that water, that dark, dark water. Blood, blood enough for six children.

October 31st 1965

Fifty years ago today.

Those that know these things — those who have studied such…supernatural events, they say that in fifty years the children will return. Not as children you understand. Fifty years in the water?…you can imagine what they'll look like. Not human. Not human at all.

But they will return to play again along the streets. They will sing the song again.

The song that casts a spell on all who hear it.

'Girls and boys come out to play
The moon doth shine as bright as day
Lose your supper and lose your sleep
Come to your playfellows in the street.'

So tonight, if you should hear that song, don't try to cover your ears with the pillows. That will never work. Don't call out to your parents — they won't be there to hear you.

Because if you hear that song, it's too late. It's just too late.

When Birthday is Death Day

Kimmie watched the car draw up. The boot lid flipped open and she stepped forward and lifted her case into the empty space. The lid closed with a click. The rear door swung open and she slid into the air-conditioned interior.

Two people were in the car — a man and a woman both wearing dark glasses — but they didn't turn to look at her. She didn't try to say hello. The door closed. She turned in her seat and looked up at her block, searching for Level 27. Were those two faces at the window? Mother and father watching her leave?

They hadn't wanted to look her in the eyes when they said goodbye. They looked at their feet instead. Her mother straightened Kimmie's rain jacket then let her hands drop. Kimmie saw the tears in her eyes. Her father was chewing his lip. They could hardly bring themselves to say, 'Good-bye, Kimmie.'

It had been the same on her last day at school — last Friday. The teacher, Miss Lee, just announced, 'Kimmie won't be with us next week. It's her birthday.'

At the end of the lesson, she took a ruler and carefully drew a red line through Kimmie's name and the row of marks in the register.

That day, the other kids didn't mention her birthday. Nor

that she wouldn't be there any more. She was just there and then she wouldn't be. Kimmie here. Kimmie gone. Just like that.

She'd heard the stories of Confiscation Day, whispered in class, in corners, but never openly talked about. Parents trying to hide their children, even trying to escape the country. The penalties they paid — the executions. The suicides — the bodies falling from tower blocks. The harbour clogged with corpses. All hastily cleaned up and removed by the authorities. All these silent deaths. And now it was her turn. Her stomach turned to water. She closed her eyes and tried to banish the terrifying images. What would the moment of death be? What would it be like? What was that pain like? Or would it be like sleep? A gradual drawing of curtains? The car wasn't speeding, just swishing along through the traffic, sweeping down through the Eastern Tunnel. Kimmie sank back into the soft seat, feeling the belt firm across here — safe, re-assuring. If only she did feel safe. If only she were somewhere else, anywhere else other than in the back of this car on this day — her birthday.

It was the way it was. She couldn't do anything about it. It. Confiscation Day. Kimmie was going to be 'confiscated'. She was the one in ten that was selected. It was just pure chance. Her name came up and she had to go.

Confiscation Day had been around a while. They had lessons about it at school, just to prepare. But no-one spoke of it. It had been a government rule brought in to control the population and ease the problem of young, unemployed people. 'Simple and effective and necessary' was the government tag line on their adverts. Most people got lucky. One in ten didn't. Kimmie just happened to be one of them.

The night before, Kimmie's young sister, Shammi, had come into her bed and cried so much it made Kimmie's pyjamas wet.

'Why do you have to go?' she'd sobbed. 'I will miss you so much.'

Kimmie had hugged her and cried too. 'I will miss you, Shammi.'

'But why? Why? Why do you have to go?'

'It's just what happens, girl. We have to accept it. I just hope you don't get unlucky when you are fifteen.'

That started another flood of tears — tears of sadness and of fear.

The car had moved out of the town and Kimmie stared at the jungle and hills and curling bays where the oily South China Sea lay. The two adults in front still hadn't spoken — their eyes were fixed on the road ahead. Kimmie wanted to look at what lay behind. She felt a strange pressure in the top of her head. Like a hand pressing down on her brain. Pressing her into the seat. Dark thoughts began to leak out: would she be killed? How would that be? What would they do? She closed her eyes but horrible images ran across her eyelids. She opened them again.

The car had turned onto a wider road when it happened. Out of a side street a young boy came running, his eyes wild with fear, waving his arms desperately and obviously screaming. His voice didn't reach Kimmie through the sound-proofed windows. He was dodging from side to side and behind him came two men in brown suits, sprinting fast. But the boy was quick and was putting distance between himself and the pursuers. He was half way across the street, right in front of them when he veered towards them. He was obviously signalling for the car to stop. He was seeking help. Refuge. The driver and the woman looked at each other. Kimmie leaned and shouted.

'Stop! Stop! Save him!'

The boy's arms were in the air and now he stood in the centre of the road looking straight at them. Just fifty metres away.

'Stop!' Kimmie screamed but was thrown back into her seat as the car accelerated. There was a dull thump from the front of the car. She saw the boy in the air, now rolling across the bonnet of the car, now smashing into the windscreen which bulged but held. Then his body was clattering over the roof. She turned and looked out of the rear window. The boy lay in a crumpled heap on the road, like a broken puppet, his limbs all wrong. A dark stain was spreading from under him.

Kimmie tried to speak. Tried to scream at the driver for deliberately running the boy down. But nothing came out.

No sound. No words.

The two men in brown suits were now in the road and the car stopped next to them. The driver wound the window down. The two men looked at him and nodded and he repeated that back to them. No words. Just recognition of a job done. The window slid up silently and the car accelerated away. In the back, Kimmie hugged herself and stared at the back of the head of the driver. The countryside swept silently by but she didn't see it any more. Just the boy's body bouncing towards her, over her, behind her. Over and over again.

The voice of the driver shook her. 'Here we are.'

They had pulled off the road and followed a new-laid road through the thick trees. A huge metal gate barred the way. With a whirr and a click it opened as the car slowed in front of it. There were wide lawns, rows of bushes and flowers that seemed to stretch forever. It was beautiful like she had never seen before.

The woman spoke again. 'Used to be a fancy golf course till the government took it over. Now it's... .' Her voice trailed away.

The car stopped outside a large white house with lots of decorations round the windows. A flight of steps led to an entrance — thick wooden doors with a sign on the door — Phoenix House — with a carved bird rising into the air.

The car pulled up outside a large, white house.

The door opened. Kimmie unbuckled and slid out. Her legs felt weak and she thought she was going to collapse. A hand gripped her arm and held her steady. The woman was there, holding her in one hand and her bag in the other. She smiled a thin smile at Kimmie.

'Okay? Here we go.'

Together, their feet stepping in time, they moved up towards the door. Like the electric gates, the doors opened and they walked through into the wide hallway. At the end was a wooden flight of stairs that led up into darkness.

The woman pressed her arm and moved Kimmie forward. There was a door on the left. The woman knocked lightly, opened it and guided her in.

Kimmie thought the room was empty. There was a desk and big leather chairs around the walls. In the corner sat a boy and he was staring at Kimmie — a strange stare, full of hope at the arrival of someone else, full of despair too.

'Someone will be along in a while. Just wait here.'

Then the door clicked and Kimmie was stranded in the middle of the room with the bag at her feet. The boy smiled weakly at her.

'Hi. I'm Eric.'

'Hi. Kimmie.'

'Nice name. Happy birthday.'

Now his smile was wider. She took him in. Jeans, t-shirt and baseball cap. He looked as if he played a lot of sport. Basketball she guessed. He pointed at the chair beside him.

'Well, this is weird, isn't it? Don't know what to expect really.' His voice was soft and had a smile in it.

'No, you're right. It is weird. Are you…scared?'

He nodded his head and his hair flopped forward. 'Of course. Who wouldn't be? We know it's going to happen but it doesn't stop you being afraid.'

There was pause that hung in the air. Kimmie wanted to tell him about the other boy. The boy in the road. But it seemed pointless. The boy had been pointless. Soon she would be too.

'So what will you miss most, Kimmie?'

Kimmie shrugged. There were too many things. 'My family. My little kid sis, Shammi. I'll even miss school, I guess.'

Eric nodded. 'Yeah, me too. School is okay mainly. Some of the teachers suck but, yeah. Loads of friends and all that stuff.'

Kimmie looked at him and could see him with a big bunch of other guys, messing around making a lot of noise, laughing a lot. The silence of the room pressed in on her.

'The thing that gets me is… .' The words were crowding in her mouth.

'What?' Eric prompted her.

'The thing is…we'll miss lots of stuff we didn't get to do.'

Eric looked down and a wave of sadness moved down his face from his eyes to his mouth.

'Yes, you're right.'

Kimmie was staring at him now and aware that she was staring. She wanted to ask him how he thought they would die. Would it be a gun? Drugs injected? A rope? The images crawled around her brain. She blinked her eyes, slow and hard and made the images go away. Try to be normal, Kimmie. This is the last chance to be normal.

'Like dating,' she continued. 'I've never been on a date with a boy.'

Eric was looking at her now. The smile returned.

'Really? Well I haven't been on a proper...date.'

Kimmie snuffled. 'Oh come on. Don't give me that. Of course you have.'

'No, I haven't. Honest. I've never really met a girl who I would want to...date. Just horsing around stuff with some girls in the group. But not...dating.'

Kimmie took a deep breath.

'It's like a big thing in your life, isn't it? The first date. You don't tell Mum and Dad and make up some excuse to go out.'

'And yours is?'

'I'm meeting my best friend in Shatin.'

'Good story. They'll believe that. Mine is... ,' Eric's eyes shone. 'Mine is...basketball practice.'

'Where do you go on a first date though?'

Eric thought for a moment. 'My older brother told me — don't go for coffee or anything. You'll be nervous and spill stuff on your clothes. He said 'cinema'. You don't have to talk all the time.'

Kimmie nodded. 'Yeah. Good idea. But what sort of film? Bet you like all those action movies with monsters and car crashes and stuff.'

'Yeah, I do but not for a first date. A comedy. It's nice to see a girl smile and laugh. It's an excuse to look at her.'

Kimmie smiled. He looked at her.

'I think that's good. Yes, comedy,' nodded Kimmie. 'You kind of share the jokes.'

'And the popcorn.'

'Eh?'

'You share the popcorn. My brother says that's when you touch the girl's hand.'

Kimmie looked at him to see if he was joking. He wasn't.

'See?' he went on. ' When both your hands go for the popcorn…'

He demonstrated by taking her hand and holding it between them, poised over the imaginary box of popcorn. 'And my hand comes here.'

And suddenly their hands were interlocked. Neither wanted to let go. It seemed natural. Neither was embarrassed.

'See?' Eric smiled again. ' Popcorn — holding hands.'

Kimmie looked down at their hands.

'Your brother seems to know a lot.'

'Not really. He's a bit of a dork.'

That pressure in the top of her brain had gone. She just

felt warm — warm from inside — sat there, holding Eric's hand. This boy she had only known a few minutes.

Kimmie's eyes looked into his.

'And what have we been talking about?'

'Oh, the usual stuff. School. Trouble we get into. Stupid friends.'

'Shopping?'

'Maybe .' He shook his head. 'Maybe not.'

'The movie?' Kimmie suggested.

'Yeah. The movie is very funny.'

And then they were in the cinema and the film was running above them.

'I like this bit.' Eric leaned his head towards her. 'Where he falls out the window.'

She turned to him and their faces were really close.

'You've seen the film before?'

'Yeah. I saw it last week.'

Kimmie moved her head back.

'Were you on a date then?'

Eric laughed. 'No! I told you. No. I was with my brother.'

'The brother who is a dork but who knows all about dating. That brother?'

'Yes. That brother.'

She leaned towards him again. 'Are you sure?'

Now he clasped her hand in both of his.

'Yes. Really. My brother.'

They were looking into each other's eyes. Kimmie wanted

to hold onto this moment forever. When Eric spoke it was more like a hoarse whisper.

'This film's not very good, is it? Do you want to watch any more?'

Kimmie's eyes searched his face.

'No. No, I don't.'

Eric leaned closer. She could feel his breath on her nose, her mouth.

'Shall we do something else instead?'

Kimmie took a deep breath and held it as if she was going to plunge underwater.

'Yes.'

She closed her eyes. She felt his lips on hers, soft at first and then harder. His hands squeezed her hand. She reached up with her other hand and touched his cheek. The kiss went on and on and now Kimmie's head seemed to be spinning for a different reason.

The door suddenly clicked open. Kimmie and Eric pulled apart and looked at the two brown-suited men in the doorway. They could have been the men she had seen chasing the boy in the street. She flinched.

'It's time. Step forward.'

Their voices were hard and rough-edged. Slowly letting go of each other's hands, the two fifteen-year-olds stood, picked up their bags and walked slowly forward. The two

KIMMIE AND ERIC PULLED APART
AND LOOKED AT THE TWO MEN IN
THE DOORWAY.

men turned and in the hallway, stepped towards the stairs. Kimmie and Eric fell in behind them.

As they slowly moved upwards, Eric's hand found Kimmie's again and hung on tight.

At the top, one of the men pointed in opposite directions.

'Boys this way. Girls that way.'

For a moment, Kimmie and Eric paused, their hands clasped. Their eyes met and lingered, just for that moment.

'See you, Kimmie. It's been nice.'

Kimmie's breath seemed to have run out completely. She blinked back something in the corner of her eyes and she smiled at him.

'It has been nice. See you.'

That's when the rough, grey bags were pulled over their heads. The sudden darkness, the bag clinging to her mouth stopping her breath, her arms being pinned behind her, threw her mind into chaos. Her heart was exploding in her chest. She tried to wrestle free from the hands that gripped her but they just span her, pressed her forward, down, towards the ground. She heard Eric's muffled voice screaming. Screaming her name.

'Kimmie! Kimmie!'

And just for a few seconds more she still existed as her name echoed round the hallway.

Day of the Water Ghosts

David Lam loved history. He hated his history teacher who always complained about David's handwriting ('too small and wriggly') and never saw David's actual history work ('your spelling is terrible'). He never saw that David loved history. He never saw David's collection of black and white photographs of Hong Kong : pictures of serious-faced people staring defiantly at the camera. They didn't smile or wave or pull faces like the selfies of today. No, they stared silently at the camera, preserving their dignity: these street traders, rickshaw runners, bricklayers. Just staring and glaring at the camera. Were they angry? thought David. Angry at having to stand still? Angry that their souls would be taken by the camera?

It was the fishermen he liked the most. The way they balanced on their boats or leaned on their poles or oared the water with their dark, sinewy arms. They were part of the sea and part of the land. They lived in both equally well. Creatures of two worlds, two elements: earth and water.

'David!' his mother's voice called. 'Dinner is ready. Come on.'

But there was one photo that always made him stop and draw it nearer to his eyes. He had bought it in a market somewhere — he couldn't remember where — there was just something about it. Something odd. Five men — fishermen — standing on their sampan, staring at the camera. Their eyes and faces seemed blank with hate. Their fists were clenched, gripping hooks and cudgels and razor — sharp gutting knives. They stood like warriors ready for the final battle. David turned the photo over — he couldn't bear them staring at him. On the back written in scratchy ink pen:

The Kismet

Tin Hau Day 1915

All souls lost.

One hundred years old, the five still looked out with stares that would burn a hole in your soul.

David had done some research. How he loved shuffling through records and documents. At first he found nothing. Few maritime records had been kept. Chinese fishermen counted for nothing in the eyes of the British overlords. But then he found a newspaper clipping at the Central Library — a short, tragic story.

'Five fishermen from Tseung Kwan O perished when their boat sank in a heavy storm on Tuesday night. It is believed they mis-read rescue signals from the village.'

That was it. A mystery. What signals were given? How could they be misunderstood?

David imagined the panic, the noise of the storm, the sampan dipping, turning foundering, trapping men, the water flooding their lungs, their desperate cries, reaching out to each other, to grasp some driftwood, then slowly, one by one, slipping below the pounding waves. On Tin Hau Day. The day to worship the Goddess of the Sea. How she had betrayed them… .

Is that why they looked so angry in the photo? Did they know something was wrong? Did they know they were going to die?

'No-one fishes today. That is it. No fishing.'

Ping, the village chief, slapped his fist on the desk. Ah Wong moved back. He knew Ping's temper and the violence that followed.

'But Ping, my brothers and I need to fish. We need the money. You know how poor we are.'

They were poor, Ah Wong thought, because they paid so much to Ping for every fish they landed. There was no choice: no pay, no fish. And now it was no fishing anyway. Ping looked at him with angry, red eyes.

'You go out and it's the last time you fish. Ever.'

Ah Wong turned slowly and walked out of Ping's dirty little cabin office. His four brothers were waiting for him outside, their faces hopeful.

'Well?'

'Ping says no fishing. Because of Tin Hau.'

Yi Wong, the biggest and strongest, stepped forward.

'Stupid superstition. No-one believes that nonsense anymore. Come on, brother Ah. We go anyway. The Wong boys aren't standing for this anymore.'

David took the photo with him to the dinner table and propped it up in front of him. His mother was pushing plates of vegetables onto the table.

'Move the photo, David. There's no room. What have you got it here for anyway?'

'It's the five fishermen.'

'Oh, not that old nonsense again. Why don't you forget them?'

David's eyes were fixed on them.

'Tomorrow is Tin Hau Day.'

His mother shrugged. 'So?'

'We should give prayers to Tin Hau. And save their souls.'

His mother snorted. 'You don't believe that rubbish, do you? Just silly old superstitions. The only way to save souls is to become a doctor. Something useful. Not just reading books. And staring at photos.'

It was no good arguing with her. Just a dead end street. But David knew. He'd read all about it in books, on line. A special prayer on the eve of Tin Hau would save their souls. And he knew what the prayer was and he knew where to go to deliver the prayer.

Before the sun was up, Ah Wong was untying the mooring rope and the other four were quietly paddling the boat forward towards the harbour opening. The boat slipped easily past the other tethered boats, calmly, quietly heading away from the sleeping village of Tseung Kwan O.

Yi Wong pulled the pile of nets out and straightened them ready to be dropped overboard.

'No fishing? Ping can go hang himself.'

In the darkness, David tiptoed out of the flat, sliding the catch silently on the front door. Down three flights of stairs and into the street. It was nearly midnight. He had to be on the fishing quay ready by then. He jogged down the street away from the cluster of housing blocks, through the rough, uneven open ground towards the concrete and wooden jetties that used to be the centre of the old fishing village.

A light wind blew in from the sea, plucking at the five orchids he carried. He checked his watch. Two minutes to spare. He slid through the gate in the high wall that once kept the jetties secure.

'Time to go to work, brothers,' said Ah Wong and five pairs of hands hauled up the nets and slid them over the side of the sampan. The boat dipped on that side and seemed to groan.

'Let's hope for a good catch.'

The sudden breeze tugged at Ah Wong's shirt, enough to make him think one of the others had pulled it as a joke.

David knew the story — the myth — the ritual — only too well. He had read it a hundred times. The souls of the dead would return after one hundred years. And this was one hundred years today. He had written out the special prayer — it was in his trembling hand or was it the wind that moved it? He pulled his torch out and clicked it on. He took a deep breath and began to read the prayer our loud, looking down into the oily, black water that lapped against the jetty.

'Tin Hau — Goddess of the Deep

This promise you must keep

As the tide and water rolls

Bring again all lost souls.'

As he read, he carefully dropped the five orchids into the water and watched them as they slid away out into the darkness, driven by the wind.

'Where the hell did this storm come from? There was no sign.'

Yi Wong was desperately clinging to the nets as the sampan plunged helplessly from wave to wave. Huge walls of water, battered up by the howling wind, swept around them as the little boat tried valiantly to ride them. But more and more water was rushing in and no matter how much the brothers bucketed water from the bilge, the boat was gradually going under.

Ah Wong stepped forward with a razor-sharp machete.

'I'll cut the nets away or they'll drag us under.'

For a moment the others hesitated. The nets had a good haul of fish. They would lose the fish and their nets. It would take weeks to make more nets. Weeks of no money.

'Cut the nets away!'

They knew Ah Wong was right as the boat see-sawed again, nearly throwing them out into the boiling waters. Their blades came down. The nets shivered, stretched and fell away, disappearing quickly. Immediately the sampan responded, riding over the waves more easily now.

'Let's head back,' shouted Ah Wong, pulling at the tiller and feeling the boat slide freely towards the dark outline of the coast. Some lights were on in Tseung Kwan O village. It seemed too early for that. Who could be up at this time? They would be back in the morning before anyone had noticed they had gone.

The wind was still thrashing up some big waves which made the boat shudder and twitch. The brothers looked at each other, their eyes showing the white of fear.

'We'll soon be in the harbour,' Ah Wong cheered them, hauling on the tiller to straighten the boat again.

That was when the boat crunched to a halt, the nose dipped and a huge wave thundered over them, throwing them all into the bottom of the boat.

'We've hit something. We've run aground!'

Yi scrambled to the front of the boat and then turned in horror.

'No, we're not aground. There's a thick wire across the harbour entrance. We're caught up on it.'

The others struggled to the front and there it was: a thick hawser caught in the wood frame of the prow of the boat.

Another wave struck and nearly took all five overboard.

'Who put that across? They've blocked the harbour! We can't get in!'

In the stormy darkness, a short way across the pounding surf, a light flickered into life and they saw Ping, standing in the circle of light on the harbour wall, watching them.

'This is his work! Ping did this to punish us!'

'Wait till I get hold of him!'

But there was no waiting. The next wave, bigger than the rest, plucked the boat up. With its prow caught in the wire, the sampan turned on its end and the wave, curling and falling, drove it below the surface, like hammering a nail into soft wood. Pinned under the falling boat, there was nowhere for the five fishermen to go except down.

Ping doused his lamp and moved away, shaking his head.

David had finished. There was just the sign of dawn in the Eastern sky — a pale orange glow — as he turned back towards the gate. His fingers scrambled with the latch to open it but the rusty mechanism wouldn't shift. The gate lock had jammed. He picked up a stone and hammered at it but caught his fingers. The pain was sharp and blood smudged the lock. He looked up. The wall was too high to climb. He was stuck there.

The sun suddenly poked a silver-white crescent over the horizon. He turned to watch it and that's when he saw the sampan bump into the jetty he had been on. He shone his torch in the boat's direction.

'It's locked! I can't get out!' he shouted at the five men who stepped onto the jetty. Then his heart jumped. There were five men, with knives and hooks and clubs in their hands. They stood as in the photograph, their eyes blazing with anger at him.

He turned to the lock again and began clawing at it. He could hear the footsteps coming closer but dare not look round. This couldn't be. He was dreaming. He would wake up in a moment. This wasn't how it was supposed to be at all. He had tried to save them. Why were they angry with him? Why would they want to harm… ?

The first blow of the machete severed his hand, leaving it clinging like a helpless piece of raw meat to the gate lock. The second blow… .

Diary of a Whampoa Kid

Monday 12th October

There is a new boy in class today. Heck. He seems very nice — a bit shy and quiet. A bit geeky I suppose. He wears glasses and in History he knew everything from hundreds of years ago. Emma laughed at him knowing so much. She is not so nice — always picking on people. I said she was being unkind about Heck. She said he must be my boyfriend then. Everyone laughed. Except Heck and me. I told her she was horrible. At the end of lunchtime all my books had been covered in glue.

Tuesday 13th October

At lunchtime I sat in the canteen with Heck. He's really nice, and in Science — well, Biology — he knew loads about the human body and the blood system. Emma came and sat with us. I feared the worst but she tried to be friendly to Heck. She asked him to join her and her friends at the cinema. But Heck said 'No thanks'. He had already arranged to go to the cinema with me. Well, he wasn't telling the truth but I said yes he was. He obviously didn't want to go with Emma. Which is surprising in some ways, as she is a very pretty girl. But perhaps she's just pretty on the outside and ugly on the inside. She left us then, looking a bit angry. At the end of lunch-break I got a school memo saying I had to go to the Principal at 2 pm. That usually means big trouble so I was a bit scared. But when I got there, the Principal said she hadn't sent the note. She was annoyed with me for wasting her time and gave me a detention. I think I knew who sent the note!

Wednesday 14th October

Got to the cinema with Heck. He wanted to see the latest horror movie — 'Twilight — Sequel 14 '. It was fine but Emma and her friends were behind us. She kept making comments about me and Heck, and even managed to get ice-cream in my hair. It was strawberry flavour — not my favourite. Heck didn't say anything and just slid lower in his seat. I wished he had spoken up but he just went very silent and buttoned up. Just before the boy kisses the girl for the first time in the film, he just got up and left. He moved so quickly I didn't get a chance to speak to him. Emma laughed a lot after that. Even during the sad bits when the boy dies.

Thursday 15th October

A bad day at school.

A very bad day. Heck was very quiet and didn't speak much. I thought maybe he didn't like me after all. But then the really bad stuff happened. Miss Lee, the Music teacher, says her mobile phone is missing from her bag and it was there at the beginning of the lesson. She gets really cranky and turns her microphone up and squeals at us to own up. Then everyone has to empty their pockets and bags onto the desks. And when I turn my bag out — there it is, her cell phone. In my bag!

I felt terrible, everyone looking at me, thinking I am a thief. I told Miss Lee I hadn't taken it but she wouldn't listen and called for the Principal.

It was all just horrible after that. I was taken out of class and as I looked back I could see Heck. He was looking very sad and he stared at Emma with a very mean look. He thought what I thought, I guess.

The Principal was very angry — almost as angry as Miss Lee. I told them I hadn't taken the darned mobile but they wouldn't listen. They called my parents to tell them, and then I was sent home to stay for three days. Miss Lee wanted me to be expelled but the Principal thought that would be a bad idea as it involved a lot of paperwork and anyway the phone itself was very old and not worth much. A bit like Miss Lee, I thought.

Friday 16th October

Last night Mom and Dad were very sad. I told them I hadn't taken the phone and I think they believed me but there wasn't much they could do. I would just have to sit it out. I thought it was very unfair and wanted someone to stand up for justice. Someone to pursue the truth until the real villain was found. But Mom and Dad preferred to watch their favourite Korean soap opera! So I gave up and went to my room.

Well, what a surprise there was waiting for me. Heck was in my room! I thought I was dreaming but no. He gave me a shy smile and said 'Hi'. I was so surprised and asked him how he'd got in and he pointed to the open window. 'But we're on the 14th floor!' I said. He said he was really good at climbing and I didn't ask any more because I was so glad to see him.

We talked a bit about what had happened in school. He said the Principal had warned everyone in assembly to look after their belongings carefully — especially the teachers — and she looked at Miss Lee who went red. Then the principal had said stuff about honesty and stealing and the girls' volleyball team. Heck said he missed me. I said I missed him. Then he kissed me and I kissed him back and it was really nice. Then Mom shouted that dinner was ready and Heck jumped up, climbed back through the window, and I watched how quickly he clambered down the wall of the block like a very fast monkey. So, he's very good at History, Biology and climbing walls. I guess he'll get a good job one day cleaning windows in a museum or a hospital.

Wednesday 21st October

It's my first day back after being suspended. Everything is pretty much the same and the rest of the class don't seem to be too bothered when I mention 'justice'. Except Heck who agrees a lot. He hasn't visited me at home again. I said maybe all the climbing had tired him out, but he said no, he'd been really busy and he did have dark rings around his eyes like he hadn't slept too much.

Emma wasn't in school. In fact she hadn't been in school

the day before either. It was quite a shock when we were all called out into the playground for a special assembly. I said maybe Miss Lee had lost her car keys or something and we all had to be searched! I think Heck laughed or maybe he coughed. Anyway a policeman was there — not one of the fat faced men who ride the little motor-bikes — a tall man with grey hair and wearing a suit. He looked like a guy who works in a bank, but I thought he must be here to deliver justice. Maybe he would arrest Miss Lee for wrongful accusations. Or arrest the Principal for keeping us all outside standing in extreme heat. But the policeman's justice didn't stretch that far.

Actually he told us that Emma was missing. We all looked at each other (except Heck who seemed to be looking at a sweet wrapper caught on his shoe), and pulled funny faces that were supposed to mean 'What's going on?' but could also have meant 'What's that horrid smell?' Yes, the policeman went on, she's been missing for two days and her parents are very unhappy so if anyone can help the police by telling them when they saw her last, that would be good. Everyone now made faces that showed they were thinking hard about Emma. Or thinking about what they'd had for breakfast. Miss Lee was probably thinking hard about where she'd left her fancy fountain pen!

But we were all pretty sad and upset that Emma was missing because something bad might have happened to her. She also might just have taken herself off for a couple of days on her own. She was that sort of girl.

Tonight, on the television news, they showed a picture of Emma and asked anyone and everyone to help find her. The same policeman was on with his bank suit and wearing a big frown. Mom and Dad asked me about Emma but what could I tell them? She's not the nicest person in the world? She's really nasty to their daughter? School life is better when she's not around? I said she's okay I guess, which means sweet nothing.

Heck texted me to say he couldn't sneak over tonight as he was not feeling too good and might not be in school tomorrow. I thought maybe his climbing shoes were being repaired!

Thursday 22nd October

There were lots of police in school today and they interviewed every kid. Well, every kid except Heck who wasn't in. There were two policemen and a woman in and out of the Principal's office all day so she spent all day walking the corridors and picking on kids who hadn't got the right uniform or who were chewing gum or just breathing in a strange way. We all hoped the police wouldn't come again, so she could return to her office and not come out.

The policewoman asked me about Emma. What was she like? Where does she go after school? Does she have friends outside school? I didn't know what to tell them. She puts glue on people's books? She sticks ice-cream in your hair in the cinema? (strawberry flavour which is especially yuuuuuuk)? She sends notes to get you into trouble with the Principal? I thought if I told them that, I would be suspect number one. So I just said I didn't know her very well, I certainly didn't understand her. But I could see the policewoman was really worried and thought something really bad had happened.

Tonight Heck came to see me again but it was late. Mom and Dad had gone to bed and I was reading some story about ancient lands and dragons and soldiers and naughty girls who spent a lot of time taking their clothes off, which was silly because the ancient lands were very cold places. Heck looked really ill with dark bags under his eyes and a white face. I told him we had to whisper and that he was in no state to climb fourteen floors but he just shrugged. He wanted to know what the police had asked and were they in school tomorrow. I told him I didn't think so. He seemed so tense and nervous so I gave him a big hug and kissed him.

Eventually he kissed me back and smiled just a little. He said he wouldn't be in school for a few days so I said I would go round and see him and I asked him where he lived but he said that was not a good idea. His parents didn't like him bringing anyone home. I thought maybe they were religious or something but he said, no they're just weird. I think some of that has rubbed off on Heck but I still like him a lot and before he left we kissed a lot more. He may be a bit odd but he's a good kisser!

Friday 23rd October

At school I got a text from Heck saying to meet him in the kid's playground on the estate. 'It is urgent'. In assembly we'd all been told not to hang around the street after school because the police thought we might be in danger. Here I was, skipping out of the Chinese History lesson to hang around (well in a playground, not the streets, so technically I was okay). I'm not very good at skipping lessons — I usually bump into the teacher whose lesson I'm skipping and have to make some feeble excuses like I have to go to the toilet urgently. But today, no teacher, so there I was in the playground, sat on a swing but feeling very self-conscious. Heck appeared and beckoned me over into the cover of some trees. He looked really bad now. His eyes were bloodshot and his lips were blue like he'd been eating a blueberry lollipop. I gave him a big hug and said he must go to the doctor. But he said no doctor could fix his problem. Only he could. He said there were things he wanted to tell me. Really important things. And he nearly started to cry. I held his hands and looked into his red eyes and wished I could make him happy. He said I had to meet him after school and it would take a long time to fix what he had to fix. He wasn't talking about a broken window or a leaky tap! I said I'd make up some story for my parents and we could meet at five back in the playground. Then suddenly a police car cruised by and Heck was gone — just like that. I hid behind a tree and watched the car go past slowly. They were definitely on the lookout for someone — maybe kids who had skipped Chinese History lessons? You could just tell.

Hello diary — again today

I don't know how I'm going to explain all this. It's more than weird. A lot more than weird and just at this moment, I'm feeling kind of sick. Sick, deep inside. Sick, so I think I'll never sleep again.

Heck and I did meet at five as we arranged. He looked even worse if that were possible. Some of his hair was missing and the gaps on his head were red raw. It looked like he had pulled his hair out in clumps. His skin had a yellow shine and when I went to kiss him, his breath was so foul I drew back for a moment and held my breath before I moved in again. This wasn't the Heck I had first met a few days ago. It was as if life was leaking out of him. Even his voice was cracked like an old man's. He just told me to follow him.

We walked as quickly as Heck's shuffle would allow. He limped badly and his back was bent so our journey was not a quick one. As we passed, people stared at the strange, sick creature stumbling along and, in the end, Heck took my scarf and wrapped it round his face. We moved from the residential area to streets where there were only store houses with vans and lorries parked outside. The area seemed deserted. Many of the buildings were no longer in use, their windows black and blank.

It was as if life was leaking
out of him.

It was outside one of these that we stopped. Heck said something about his father owning it but there was no notice or sign on the front door. He took out a key and a moment later we were out of the bright sunlight and in a dark, musty corridor. He clicked a switch and rows of lights came on. Just for a moment he touched my arm and looked at me and I saw the old Heck — not this strange, awkward old thing. I wanted to just hold him and keep him safe from whatever was happening to him but he turned and moved away.

We went up four or five flights of stairs. I lost count. With each set of stairs Heck seemed to weaken. His breathing was heavy and he leaned against the wall before he could climb again.

Eventually we stopped climbing and followed a corridor to a door at the end. Heck looked at me and said sorry with a very sad look on his face as if he were saying goodbye for the last time. In a way he was, I discovered later.

He unlocked the door and drew me through. The room had been an office I guessed from what I could see in the half light. Then he turned the light on.

Emma was in a chair behind the desk. She was chained to it, the chains passing round her body two or three times. She was wriggling to get out as soon as the light came on. But it was her face I stared at. The pretty face was no more — it was just a mask of fear. Her eyes were swollen and tears streamed down. Her nose flooded her mouth with snot. Her mouth sagged open and she dribbled helplessly. As Heck moved towards her, Emma's eyes rolled around and she started moaning — not screaming or crying — just moaning, a horrible sound that seemed to come from deep inside her. Heck reached out and rested his hand on her and the moaning quietened. Then he began talking, quietly at first, as if he were piecing together a jig saw story.

'I'm sorry,' he said to me then turned to Emma. 'And I'm sorry to you, Emma.'

She just rolled her eyes again. He looked at me.

'I need to trust that you will understand me and what I have to do.'

He was looking at me again. I was silent. No words would come. How could I begin to understand what he had done to Emma. He tried to stand upright.

'I am dying. I will die in a few hours. I know that. So I have to tell you. I am a dracula — a vampire you would say. I have lived like this, in the same body, for many years. Many years.'

Things about him dropped into place.

'But I have reached my sanguina — my crisis point — and I need blood.'

Emma shuddered and kicked against the desk.

'I took Emma because…she deserved it.' He turned to her and she was suddenly still with terror. 'You were not a good person. I thought it better to take you for what I needed.'

Emma shook her head and began moaning but Heck put his fingers to her lips and she became quiet.

'But then I realised it was you I really wanted.'

Heck was looking at me and his eyes were shining for a moment.

'And if it's you I take — you will be with me forever. It's the blood, you see. I need the blood. The blood gives me life and stops the sanguina.'

He paused and his body slumped a little. He was still staring at me.

'Well? Will it be you or Emma? What do you want?'

I looked at Emma who was staring at me too, her mouth wide open but silent.

'If you choose me, what about Emma?' I asked.

Now Emma's face had a dreadful, pleading expression. Heck shook his head.

'She knows everything. What can I do?'

His voice was a thousand years of death and torture and cruelty. If I said yes I would join him in that world. He raised his hand towards me — beckoning my answer.

Well, dear Diary. This is perhaps the last time I write in you. Everything has changed. Everything. It's like I've passed over into another world. The dark side.

I'll have to wear a scarf every day to hide these two small holes in my neck. I've bought a lot of different scarves and some of them are really nice. Emma likes wearing them too. And as for Heck. Well, in the end, boys are all the same aren't they? So selfish. And that is so uncool.

HIS VOICE WAS A THOUSAND YEARS OF CRUELTY AND TORTURE.

The Baby Business

Lily looked at herself in the mirror. She did look pregnant. Really pregnant and she felt really pregnant. Her whole body was a heavy weight she was trying to move around. And inside there — she clutched her swollen stomach — was a baby. Someone who she would have to look after for the rest of her life perhaps. She didn't know whether to laugh with joy or cry in despair.

How had this happened? How had she got to this crazy point in her life ? At fifteen years of age ? Oh she remembered the start of it. Oh yes. Joey and his eighteen year old smile. Joey the cool guy who smoked and drank alcohol and stayed out on the streets till early morning every day. Joey the cool guy. Who walked away shaking his head, when she'd told him the news that he was going to be a father.

Things just went from bad to worse after that. Telling Mum and Dad had not been easy. Their reaction had been harder to take. They put her straight into one of the special hostels for young women, her father dropping her pathetic little case on the doorstep and then he walked off without looking back. So there she was, on her own, among all these older girls who were nearly all pregnant. Oh she had a room which she shared with two other girls — a room with a window which looked out at a blank wall. A bed. A box for her possessions. That was it. It was a government hostel so there was congee for breakfast and a hot meal, usually meat and vegetable stew, every night. The doors were locked at 9 pm.

The days were worse than the nights. Lily wandered the streets of Mongkok and Tsim Sha Tsui begging. Sometimes she just sat on the pavements with her hands held out. Sometimes she just stood there and asked passing strangers for coins. Sometimes old men came up to her and whispered dirty things in her ear. Yes it could mean money but she just spat at them. They walked away laughing or they smacked her head with a heavy hand. A few people dropped coins or maybe a 20 dollar note into her hands but most people walked past her as if she didn't exist. Their eyes were full of pity or shame or anger. There was never a friendly word. Never.

Soon everything would change though. She wouldn't be alone anymore. She would have a baby. Her baby. And they would be in the world together. And perhaps Lily would find happiness.

It was a boy. The nurse called Noi smiled when she told Lily, as she wrapped the new baby, all red and shiny, in a clean white towel. Noi was still smiling when she carried Boy towards the door.

'Can I hold him Nurse Noi?'

Noi's smile flickered and died. Her face creased with

alarm.

'Lily I can't. You're not allowed to hold the baby. You're not even supposed to see the baby'.

Lily's hands reached out towards Noi. Towards Boy.

'What do you mean? It's my baby. Let me hold him?'

Noi turned the baby away from Lily.

'It's the rules. It's the Law, Lily. You can't see the baby. That's it. It belongs to….the Company now.'

Lily put out both her hands now, flicking them at Noi.

'What are you talking about, Noi? I just want to hold the baby.'

Noi took another step towards the door.

'Lily, the Company owns the baby. Not You. He will go to a good home. He will be well looked after.'

The nurses' words were cutting into Lily's heart. She wanted to tear the baby down from Noi's hands and rush from this place.

'Noi, I thought you were my friend. Not just my nurse. You've looked after me for two months. We are friends. How can you do this to me?'

Noi reached forward and closed the door, pressing it quietly closed. Her eyes met Lily's and they were brimming with tears.

'Lily I'm so sorry. It's what I have to do. I have no choice. The baby always goes to the Company. And, you know, the Company owns all of Hong Kong. It can do whatever it likes.'

'Including stealing my baby?'

'It's not stealing your baby. It's being…redistributed.'

Now tears were filling Lily's eyes.

'Redistributed? What does that mean? You mean someone else will have my baby? Not me? Why not me? It's mine? No-one said this would happen. Why wasn't I told? I would have run away'

Noi shook her head.

'It wouldn't have been any good, Lily. We are not allowed to tell you. They would have searched for you, found you, punished you. There is no escaping not with the Company.'

Lily looked around, her eyes wide with fear and crazy ideas.

'We don't have to do this, Noi. We can hide the baby. You can say it didn't live. That you got rid of it. You can do that, Noi, can't you? The company will never know.'

'Lily. The Company knows everything. They see everything. Even now. Us. Here. They are watching.'

Lily's eyes cast desperately around to see anyone watching. Cameras pointing. Nothing. Just the empty room and Noi's sad expression.

'What will the Company do with my baby, Noi?'

Noi looked away.

'Noi. What will they do with my baby? Will they…kill it? Will they kill my baby?'

Noi shook her head.

'No. Nothing like that. Your baby will be looked after. Well looked after at…the farm.'

The word pounded into Lily's head.

'Farm? Farm? What sort of farm? A baby farm? What the hell is that?'

Noi bit her lip and looked away.

'They do things there. Oh, it will be fine, Lily. Please believe me.'

But Lily's hands were on Noi, dragging her close.

'Tell me, Noi. Tell me. What is the farm? What do they do? What do they do at the farm?'

'It's to help science. Medical science. Research. It's to help all of us.'

'You mean experiments, don't you? They are going to experiment on my baby? They are going to…'

'Shut up, Lily. Not so loud. No-one is supposed to know. I shouldn't have told you.'

'Oh Noi. Please don't let this happen. You can do something. We can do something. You don't have to do this thing, do you? You can help me. Help us?' Noi's eyes fixed on Lily's eyes. Both sets of eyes were welling up with tears. Suddenly Noi reached forward and took Boy from Lily's arms.

'Follow me Lily. Bring your bag.'

Lily slid off the bed — she was hurting, hurting everywhere in her body but she knew she had to go. Her bag was by her bed filled carelessly with the few things of her life — a comb, a washbag, a face flannel. She held it to her as if it were Boy and followed the blue uniformed back of Noi.

NOI'S EYES FIXED ON LILY'S EYES.

Noi was walking slowly, trying to be natural and Lily followed, head down, not wanting to catch the eye of anyone passing. A nurse passed in the opposite direction, staring at a paper in her hand. Ahead a doctor was leaning forward talking to someone in a bed.

'This way.' hissed Noi, changing direction and pushing through a door marked 'Staff only'. Lily followed.

The passage beyond was dark. Stairs reached steeply upwards. Noi didn't pause but pressed on up the steps. Lily grabbed the hand rail and hauled herself upwards.

'Where are we going? Noi?'

'Don't ask, just follow.'

Lily's legs felt weak with the effort of climbing. Her breath leaked from her. Noi was getting further away.

'Noi! Slow down. I don't feel so good.'

Noi stopped, turned and looked down. She smiled as an apology.

'Sorry, Lily. It's okay, just keep going.'

Now Lily was at her heels, rising higher, higher up this dark funnel in the hospital.

'Not far now, Lily.'

And then they stood in front of a door. Noi took a deep breath and looked at Lily.

'Where are we Noi? What's beyond the door?'

Noi smiled but was it a natural smile? Lily looked again into her eyes. Were they smiling too?

'It's okay, Lily. Open the door. You go first.'

SOMETHING WAS WRONG — SHE WAS SURE.

Lily hesitated.

'But where…?'

'Just open the door, Lily and step through.'

Lily reached out her free arm which wasn't clutching the bag.

'Can I take Boy, then?'

Noi turned a little from her.

'No, I'll carry him through. Open the door and through you go.'

Lily stared at the door handle. Her head pounded. Her heart was throbbing. Something was wrong — she was sure. Her hand hovered over the door handle.

'But Noi, I'm not….'

Noi's hand crashed down on top of hers, knocking the door handle forcibly downwards. Lily felt the weight of Noi's shoulder pushing against her back. She fell forwards into the door which crashed open. Lily couldn't keep her feet. She was falling helplessly forwards, her bag spilling ahead of her.

Bright white light flooded into her eyes, blinding her, burning her. She hit the floor and scrambled to look back. The floor was hot. There was a strange smell in the air. Hot metal and burning. A sweet, slightly sickening smell. The floor beneath her was sticky.

'Noi! What are you doing?'

She saw Noi's face in the doorway. Noi was shaking her head. There was a look of pity in her eyes. She saw Boy's face, staring out, trying to understand what was happening. She flung her arms out towards him, trying to grasp him back but Noi inched back just out of reach. Lily gasped and fell to the floor again. The surface was hotter still and she tried to get up as the pain burned into her. Then the door slammed tight and she saw them no more. She looked down at her hands and saw the skin puckering and splitting into red sores. The searing pain in her feet threw her whole body into a spasm. A scream welled in her throat but became a muffled gargling as darkness descended.

Noi passed slowly back down the ward corridor towards where she had been a few minutes before. The doctor was now at the bed where Lily had been. He lifted the medical record, then looked at Noi and the baby in her arms.

'Everything all right, Nurse Noi?' His voice was calm and matter of fact.

Nurse Noi nodded.

'Yes Doctor. Job complete. Another boy.'

'Well done, Nurse. Good work. Good Company work.'

Spirite

(Based on a traditional Chinese ghost story, 'The Taoist Monk'.)

'Who is that weird girl? She's new isn't she?'

'Do we have to put up with even more weirdo geeky kids at our school?'

Cindy and Char (so much neater than Charlotte, she thought) were staring at the girl standing at the school snack bar. She was wearing school uniform but it didn't look the same as theirs. The jumper was big and baggy. Theirs were neat and tight to show they were real girls. The blouse collar was big. She had ankle socks that made her legs look thick — not like the white knee-lengthers they wore. And her hair! It was pulled back tightly into a bun at the back. A bun! Not even a pony tail or a pineapple.

'She looks like my Mum must have been at school,' grinned Candy.

'More like your Dad, actually. She's weird alright,' confirmed Char.

At that moment the girl had turned and seen them looking at her. She smiled and started to walk towards them.

'Oh my God,' muttered Cindy. 'Don't look. She's coming our way.'

'Let's go,' said Charlotte rising from the table.

'Too late, Char,' said Cindy.

And the girl was there in front of them, clutching an orange juice and a fish-ball stick.

'Hi, you two. Mind if I join you?'

And before they could say, 'No way. This table is for the cool crowd,' she was there.

Cindy and Char sat for a moment. Their mouths open, staring at the newcomer. They couldn't quite believe that she had come over and spoken to them. To them! The coolest dudes in school. No-one spoke to them unless invited.

'Wha…nooo…bu…,' jabbered Cindy.

'Ba…whooo…you…,' slobbered Char.

'Thanks,' smiled the girl.

She sat opposite them, still smiling at them.

'I'm Spirite. It's spelt i-t-e but you say 'itay'. Spirite.'

'Spirite,' chanted Cindy and Char in unison.

'Yes, that's right. How clever of you. And you must be Cindy and Charlotte.'

'Char,' corrected Charlotte, annoyed at having her full name spoken and doubly annoyed at hearing her name being spoken by this…weirdo freak newbie.

'My teacher — Miss Chan — said to look out for you two.'

Cindy and Char looked at each other. 'She did, did she?'

Spirite laughed. 'Oh, not like that, I'm sure. She meant I was bound to meet you. Not that you were…trouble or anything.'

Their two pairs of eyes turned on her like searchlights. Their mouths were still slack. Spirite bumped her juice on the table in front of them and sat smiling.

'Well, I'm the fresher…the new girl,' she began.

'Newbie,' cut in Cindy. 'You're the newbie.'

'Newbie,' Spirite repeated. ' Yes, I get it.'

'I don't think you do, newbie girl,' said Cindy and there was a cold edge to her voice this time. Her mouth had stopped drooping in disbelief.

But the newbie's eyes were on the bag of pretzels that the two girls were sharing.

'Mmm. They look nice,' the girl said, ' May I…?'

And before Cindy or Char could speak in protest, Spirite had reached out and taken one, popped it in her smiling mouth and crunched it.

'They taste great. What are they?'

Cindy stared hard at the girl in front of her. Was she for real? Who did she think she was, coming here speaking to them, eating their pretzels?

'They're pretzels. They're called pretzels.'

Spirite was still crunching noisily.

'Mmm. They are nice.'

'Yes, they are nice,' repeated Cindy tonelessly.

'Do you mind if I…?' And Spirite's fingers closed on another pretzel and the noisy crunching continued.

'I think we'll be in the same Math group. And English. And Chinese History. That'll be fun. The three of us.'

'The three of us?' chorused Cindy and Char.

'Yes. For sure. The three of us.'

'Well, I'm the ...fresher... the new girl.'

The two friends — who everyone else knew at school as the High Cees — looked at one another, looked away, looked at the newbie then back at each other.

'But we're… .'

'It's not like… .'

'I don't think… .'

But nothing got to be finished. And Spirite was still smiling. Suddenly she stood up, drained the orange juice in one swig, gnawed the final fish-ball off the stick and stepped away from the table.

'Gotta go, girls. Need to check out the Library. See you later.'

And Spirite bounced away between the tables. There was a pause. The two girls seemed to be recovering their breath, unable to speak. Finally Cindy's words broke through.

'Who does she think she is?'

Char was spluttering, red-faced. 'She's a newbie! She's a freak! A geek!'

'She's so…so…such…bad manners… .'

Cindy shook her head in disbelief. 'Just avoid her next time. Ignore her. Spirite.' (she exaggerated the 'ay' sound). 'What sort of name is that?'

Char shook her head. 'She's a freak alright.'

Her tongue caught against something sharp on her teeth. 'Ugh! I just lost a filling.'

At the end of the school day, Cindy and Char headed down to the mall to Starbucks — their favourite 'willing-to-

' She's a freak, alright!'

be-chilling' place. The cappuccinos frothed white in front of them. This was their cool little paradise.

'Hi, girls. Thought you might be here.'

Their blood and their faces froze as Spirite flopped onto the leather sofa between them.

'This is a really nice place,' she said, looking around her with a smile. 'That drink looks good. What is it?'

'Cappuccino,' the two spoke together.

'It's coffee,' added Char, feeling she was speaking to a four year old.

'Cappuccino,' Spirite repeated slowly then dipped her finger into the two cups and licked the milk froth from it. 'Yes, it is good. I'll try that next time. You are teaching me so much. Pretzels. And now cappuccino.'

Cindy had a horrid vision of what the next time might be.

'The next time?'

The girl was still smiling. There was a bubble of froth on her chin.

'Yes. Next time I'm here with you. I haven't got time right now. I've got to check out the public library.'

As she stood she caught the table with her knee. Coffee juddered out onto the table top.

'Oh, sorry. Bye Cindy. Bye Char.'

And she was gone.

Cindy slapped her knee in anger and frustration.

'I can't stand this. She's awful.'

'She thinks we're her friends.'

'She thinks…she thinks…we…like her!'

'She's such a freak!'

The little pool of coffee had dribbled down onto Cindy's white socks. She gasped at the row of little brown stains.

'My socks! They're ruined! Oh… oh…!'

Char was on her feet. 'Let's get out of here before she comes back.'

The next day there had been no sign of Spirite at school. Cindy and Char supposed she was absent or busy finding libraries. After school they headed for the shops, not risking a visit to Starbucks again in case…well, just in case. H&M seemed fairly empty and Zara was the same. They wandered the racks of clothes, idly dragging their fingers across the tops and skirts and skinny jumpers. Nothing really took their fancy and they had no money on them so it didn't matter. Suddenly Candy froze.

'Oh no. Over there in the doorway. Her! Get down!'

Cindy pulled Char into a crouch behind a row of trouser bottoms. They stared hopelessly as a pair of feet wearing black, sensible sandals appeared in front of them.

'Hi, Cindy. Hi, Char. What are you doing down there? Have you lost something?'

Slowly the two rose. Cindy covered one eye with her hand.

'I think I've lost a contact lens.'

Spirite looked puzzled. 'A what lens? You mean your

spectacles?'

'My contact lens,' repeated Cindy, unable to process the question. 'But oh no… .' (forcing a smile) '…it's here safe and sound.'

Char was staring at Cindy's eye.

'But you don't… .'

'It's safe, thank goodness,' hissed Cindy, looking hard at Char. 'My lens is safe.'

Char nodded unsurely. 'Oh, good. It's safe.'

Spirite was flicking through the clothes. 'I just hope I never have to wear glasses. They'd make me look stupid.'

Cindy smirked. 'You don't need glasses to do that.'

The girl was holding up a pair of bright pink trouser pants with a big 'Sale Price' ticket dangling.

'Do these look nice?'

Char looked at Cindy and pulled a sucking lemons face. 'Yes. Very smart. Buy them.'

Cindy snuffled. 'You'd look cool in those.'

Spirite smiled. 'Okay. If you say so. If you think they'd look smart.'

And Spirite was off to the changing room, clutching the garment under her arm.

Cindy grabbed Char. 'We've got to tell her.'

Char grabbed Cindy. 'You tell her. She thinks we're her best friends. You've got to tell her or she'll be with us everywhere.'

Spirite returned wearing the pink bottoms and a big,

positive smile.

'Well? What do you think? Are they okay?'

The girls looked at each other then at her.

'Well,' began Cindy.

'They are,' continued Char.

'But you're not.'

Spirite peered at them. 'Do you mean I don't suit them?'

Cindy shook her head. 'No. We mean, you don't suit us. You're not...one of us.'

Char chimed in. 'You're not a new friend for us. You're just a...newbie nobody. And we'd rather you didn't talk to us.'

'Or do anything around us,' added Cindy for good measure.

Spirite looked at them in turn and the smile shrank from her face.

'So,' Cindy stretched the word out. 'Just leave us alone. Okay?'

Unsure of how Spirite might react, Char grabbed Cindy's arm and dragged her away. Spirite watched them leave the shop. She heard some of their muttered words: 'weird...' 'freak...' 'loser...'. She looked down at her pink legs and thought how stupid she looked. How very, very stupid.

As Char left her blouse snagged on a clothes rail and the sleeve tore. 'Oh hell! It's ruined,' she whined, holding the tear in place.

The next day at school, there was no sign of Spirite. Cindy breathed a deep sigh of relief.

'I'm glad we told her straight.'

'She won't bother us again. Did you see her face when I told her?'

And yet there was something about the girl that was… different. They couldn't work out what it was. She seemed to be from another planet. She didn't know things. The way she talked was odd. They tried to dismiss her from their thoughts. But she wouldn't go, especially when they found a pink envelope on their desk in the English lesson. Carefully they opened it. There was a card inside, with a single red rose on the front. Inside, neat handwriting spread across both sides of the card.

Dear Cindy and Charlotte

I'm sorry I upset you. You seemed so nice and friendly. You don't have to be my friends but I would like you to come to a party at my house on Saturday night. It will be fun, I promise. 141 Oxford Road. Kowloon Tong. 8 pm. Hope you can make it.

Spirite X

Cindy stared at the card. 'She's joking, isn't she? A party?'

Char giggled. 'Bet it's a party where we sit around reading books.'

'Wearing pink pants.'

But then their thoughts hurried on into Mischief Land.

'Actually,' Cindy was smiling, 'I'm not doing anything on Saturday night. Are you?'

Char took out her cell and carefully checked the calendar.

'Do you know what?' She was grinning too. 'Neither am I. I think we can go to Spirite's party. It could be fun.'

141 Oxford Road, Kowloon Tong was not what Cindy and Char expected. It was huge. High walls with elaborate carved figures along the top. Electric gates. An intercom for security. It was 8.05. Saturday night. Cindy pressed the button.

'Cindy and Charlotte for the…party.'

A tinny voice, but quite recognisable as Spirite's, sounded.

'Oh good! You've come. Walk right in.'

The gates clicked and silently slid back revealing a garden with small blossom trees and bushes. A wide gravel path led up to front doors with fancy pillars on each side. Their feet crunched on the stones so they tried to walk more lightly.

As they got to the heavy front door, it opened and Spirite was there, smiling at them. But this wasn't the Spirite they knew. They stared at her. This Spirite was wearing a red silk dress as if she was dressed for a prom. Cindy and Char looked at their own clothes — t-shirts and jeans — and felt distinctly untidy. Spirite's hair was no longer in a bun but hung like a black fan on her shoulders. She looked — they both thought it but didn't say it — beautiful.

'Come on. Don't stand there staring.'

So they walked, staring. The house was big inside: a staircase swept from the wide hall-way. Statues and paintings lined the walls. The carpet was soft and deep beneath their feet.

Cindy was in awe. 'It's an…amazing place.'

Char was staring at a statue that seemed to be staring back at her. 'Yes, amazing.'

Spirite opened some double doors to a big room with tall windows that had heavy curtains hanging down. The furniture was leather, the tables dark, old wood.

'Who else in coming, Spirite? People from school?'

Spirite smiled, took their hands and drew them into the middle of the room.

'No. Just you two. And some other…sort of friends of mine.'

She walked behind a sofa to a table full of bottles and glasses.

'But first you must try my drink. Much better than…what is that coffee you drink?'

'Cappuccino.'

'Yes. Much better than that.'

Cindy frowned. 'Is it alcohol? We can't drink it you know. Our arms and legs go red and itchy.'

Char cut in. 'And I get sick.'

Spirite laughed. 'No. It's not alcohol or anything like that. It's just a drink to make you happy.'

She produced three glasses of a light green liquid and handed them one each. The third she took herself, put it to her lips and drained the glass.

'Ha! That's the way to drink it.'

Cindy and Char looked at each other. They couldn't do any less than the girl they despised and mirrored each other, throwing the drink down their throats. The drink seemed to taste of many things — honey, sugar, passion fruit — many, many flavours. Was that even coffee in the taste? Almost immediately they felt a gentle warmth. The tastes lingered in their mouths, now peppermint, now vanilla, now chocolate.

Cindy grinned and handed her empty glass back to Spirite.

'Yes, I like that.'

The girl in the red dress leaned forward with a wicked grin. 'Want another?'

And there they were knocking back a second drink. Then a third.

'What's it called? It's soooo nice.'

'Nectar, we call it. The drink of the gods.'

'Nectar,' echoed Char. 'I like it!'

Spirite twirled away from them, the red dress swishing against her legs.

'Let's have some music.'

She skipped over to the wall and pressed a button on a small black box and music flooded the room — a bass sound that the girls felt through the floor and the sofa they sat on. They watched as Spirite began to dance to the music, swaying, twisting, turning, stepping in, out, behind.

Cindy laughed out loud. 'Spirite! You can dance. We thought you were just a nerd.'

And she jumped up to join her.

Char was laughing too — her head full of the music, the movement, the moment. She too felt pulled into the dance.

'It feels so great!' What was in that drink?' howled Cindy, spinning round Spirite.

'It's not the drink. It's your own life that's pouring out,' called the girl in red, moving towards the doors where she stood poised, holding the handles.

'And now for some boys!'

Cindy and Char screamed together.

'What do you mean? What boys? There are boys? Who? Where?'

Spirite flung the doors open and three boys were in the doorway. They wore identical grey suits, redshirts that matched the hostess's dress and they moved forward together.

'They are so fit!' exclaimed Char.

A moment later the three girls were paired off, dancing frantically with the boys, smiling wide smiles at each other. This was better than their wildest dreams. How did Spirite — that weirdo — manage all this?

They all drank more of the happy drink; they all danced and shouted and danced some more. The music roiled out

Three boys were in the doorway.

endlessly, driving them on faster and faster. The boys' smiles flashed: the girls' eyes shone.

Suddenly the bubble burst. Spirite had pressed another button and the pounding music faded, replaced by a sweeter, slower sound — the sound of space or an undersea world — quiet swirls of music that seemed to wash like gentle waves through the air.

Spirite moved to her partner, took his hand and guided him to a sofa at the back of the room. They slid together and lay holding each other, their lips sealed together, not caring about anything or anyone else in the room. She broke the kiss for a moment and looked across at the other two girls.

'Come on, you two. We're friends forever.'

Cindy and Char watched her for a few moments.

'I think I like that idea,' said Cindy turning to the boy she was with.

'Me too,' agreed Char, looking up into the handsome face of her partner.

They moved with the boys to the other sofas, stretched out and pulled the boys to them. This was much more than they'd ever expected.

As soon as they lay back, clutching the boys, their heads seemed to spin. Was it the effect of the drink? The dancing? The boys themselves? Desperately they tried to make sense of what was happening. The room was turning, the floor seemed to slip away. Was it the music or the boys lifting them? Moving them. Everything was out of focus.

Their eyes were closing. Sleep, like a heavy blanket, was covering them and they felt themselves falling, falling into a darkness they'd never known before.

'Look at those silly bitches — la!'

The harshness of the voices, the sharpness of the laughter, dragged them back from the darkness. Where were they? It was daylight. Bright daylight. What time was it? Where were they? For a moment they thought they were dreaming. They were locked inside some strange dream.

It was the coldness of the mud they lay in that told them this was real. The mud that covered them from head to foot. The mud that lay at the bottom of the building site they were in.

Cindy tried to stand but her feet slithered and she fell, her hands plunging up to the elbows in the brown ooze.

'Where the hell are we? What happened?'

Char was trying to help pull Cindy up but she too fell, grappling and wrestling with the slippery slime they seemed caught in.

It was a building site. Heaps of bricks and stone and wood lay all around. Three workers in yellow helmets had just entered and were laughing at their efforts to stand up.

'Come on, girls. Stand up! Get moving!'

'That'll teach you to trespass!'

'Hurry up or we'll concrete you in.'

No-one came to help them. Cindy, finally pulling her

grappling and wrestling with the
slippery slime

arms free, began to cry, great big tears washing white lines in her muddy face. A moment later, Char was crying too as, on hands and knees, they crawled towards the workers and the entrance.

'You can do better than that! Come on!' jeered the three men.

When they reached solid ground the girls stood. Their shoes were gone. Their clothes were plastered to them. Their hair hung in rats' tails. Cindy looked up, tears flowing, at the man who stood at the front, his thick arms folded, his ugly face grinning.

'Where are we? What is this place?' Her voice was thin with rage and humiliation. The men laughed loudly again.

'It's on the entrance there. You must have seen it before you broke in for your mud bath.'

'Look!' shouted another, pointing to the sign. 'It says 'No Hippos'!'

The two girls trudged through the laughter to the construction site board and read the thick black letters.

No Entry
Building Site : 141 Oxford Road
Hard Hats Must Be Worn

Cindy and Char looked at each other and burst out crying again.

Monday morning. Cindy and Char were back in school uniforms, standing at the school gate. Cindy was simmering with anger.

'Wait till that bitch turns up. I'll tear her eyes out.'

Char shook her head. 'I still don't know how she tricked us. It must have been something in the drink. Did we imagine those boys? Did we just imagine it all?'

'All I know is,' hissed Cindy, 'she is going to pay big time.'

But no Spirite appeared. Many other students did and many laughed at the girls as they passed.

'Love the pictures on Facebook.'

'Enjoy the mud, did you? It's very good for the skin.'

Cindy snarled back at them. 'What are you talking about?'

And then it dawned on her. Not only had they been tricked but they had been tricked publicly. Everyone knew.

Heads down they shuffled away to their classroom and sat, surrounded by sniggering and pointing fingers. Unable to bear it, Cindy snapped at Char, 'Let's go find her in Miss Chan's class.'

They headed off to the class which was in another block. Miss Chan sat at her desk, straight-backed, looking down at the register on her lap-top.

'Excuse me, Miss Chan…,' Cindy began.

Miss Chan looked up and frowned.

'It's Cindy…and Charlotte, from…4E? What can I do for you?'

Cindy nodded. 'Yes, Miss. Has Spirite registered this morning? We missed her and wanted to find her before class. An urgent message from her mother.'

Miss Chan looked more closely at them as if she were checking that they were really there.

'Spirite?'

Someone in the class sniggered.

'Spirite?' repeated Miss Chan.

Char burst out. 'Spirite. Yes, Spirite. That's her name. Spirite!'

Miss Chan shook her head slowly.

'There's no-one in this class called Spirite. Anyone's nick-name here?'

Rows of faces grinned. Several laughed out loud.

'What a stupid name. Who would have a name like that?'

Cindy stepped forward and grabbed the lap-top, turning it to read the list.

'She said she was in this group. Miss Chan's group.'

Miss Chan pulled the lap-top away from her.

'There's no Spirite in this class for the last time. Perhaps she's in someone else's class. Now go back to your own class and register properly.

Cindy banged the teacher's desk.

'Of course, there's a Spirite! We went to her house. We...'

Her voice trailed away.

'Was it a mud house, Cindy?' someone shouted from the

back.

Cindy and Charlotte, tears falling again, turned and left, slamming the door behind them. Their screams and wails echoed through the corridors, screams of humiliation, screams of anger. And, as it dawned on them, they became screams of terror.

'We're friends forever.'

The Vampire on the MTR

Why hadn't she noticed it before? How stupid. Stupid. She must have caught stupid, like a cold, at school today. That was seven hours ago. Here it was — twelve o'clock — midnight. Alone and on an MTR station. Alone. That never happens. You are never alone on an MTR station. There is always someone else waiting — some late night person like her, making their way home to their box-in-the-sky.

Candy looked up the platform to the left at the gaping dark hole of the tunnel. Then she looked to the right — the black semi-circle which would swallow her up in a minute or so and carry her away to Yau Ma Tei.

She strained to listen for footsteps or for the distant rumble of the train getting nearer. But there was nothing — just this wall of silence building up around her. She coughed to break the silence. Her cough bounced round the walls, bounced off the adverts for white teeth and the latest movie, bounced away down the tunnel. Nothing. No-one came. No-one. She looked up at the electronic board.

'Yau Ma Tei   4 minutes'

Four minutes! Time was standing still. She checked it against her black and white Polo watch. Four minutes to midnight. She began humming a tune. She didn't know what it was — it could be anything or nothing — just to fill the silence in her head that pressed against her ear drums.

Three minutes.

She shuffled her feet, trying out a dance routine she was practising at lunchtimes with her friends. Heel, toe, heel, toe and spin. She froze and looked up at the platform camera. Perhaps someone was watching her on a telescreen somewhere, laughing at her twitching feet.

Two minutes. Now her nose was itching — it must be the dust down here underground. She dug out a tissue from her bag then sneezed like a cat, wiped her nose and dropped the tissue.

'Candy, don't be a litter dog, leaving your mess everywhere.'

Her mother's voice spoke to her in her head. She looked around and pressed her foot over the damp tissue.

'Stop trying to cover things up, Candy.'

This time it was her Dad's voice in her head.

She bent and picked up the tissue and pressed it in her bag.

One minute.

She went up on her toes, feeling the muscles in her legs tighten. She took a deep breath and held it. Stay like this till the train comes she told herself.

A voice shattered the silence. Her heart leaped and she overbalanced onto her heels.

'The twelve o'clock train to Yau Ma Tei has been cancelled. All passengers make their way to the exit. We apologise for this inconvenience.'

Cancelled? Cancelled? How could she get home? She didn't have any money for a taxi. The buses didn't run to where she lived. *Ma fan!* What could she do? She stared around as if a big notice would appear and tell her what to do.

The display unit clicked to black. Somewhere doors were shutting. She had to go. There was no choice.

She snatched her bag onto her shoulder, but too quickly. She hadn't closed it properly. Her purse, pink and yellow and her blue cell phone span through the air, landed on the edge of the platform then clattered down onto the line, out of sight.

'Ho chun! Ho chun!'

She stamped her foot in anger, stepped to the edge and looked down. The purse was in reach but the phone had bounced to the other side of the rail. She muttered a nasty word, knelt on the platform edge and reached down. Her fingers dangled out of reach of the purse.

'Oh you stupid thing! Come here!'

But it didn't. Now she had to lay on the platform — where thousands of dirty feet had walked that day. All that dirt on her best t-shirt.

'Aai-yaah!'

Her fingers scrabbled at the purse, scratched at it to bring it closer. Then she had it in her hand. But the phone? She looked up and down. Who would see her if she went on the rails? She looked at the cold, grey metal on its bed of stones. Which was the live rail? This one or that one? If she touched the live one she knew she was dead. Was it worth it for a cell phone? She could buy a new one tomorrow maybe. No, leave the phone. Leave the damned thing. Just get out of the station. Find a way home.

Candy jerked the bag back onto her shoulder and looked at the cell phone. Was it flashing? Was someone trying to ring her? She could jump down and get it.

'The station is now closed.'

The automatic, toneless voice broke her plan apart. She began running.

She ran along the platform, back through the entrance, along the corridor, the adverts on the walls a blur as she rushed. She turned a corner to get onto the escalator but the steps were still. At the top of the stair a thick metal wire mesh had dropped.

'Oh no! Not yet!'

She pounded up the sharp, heavy steps and threw herself at the gate.

'Open up! Open up! I'm still in here! Open up!'

She listened for a human voice. She listened for a door being opened. She expected some chubby man in a blue uniform to come waddling towards her. But no-one came. Not a chubby man. Not a thin man. No one.

'Let me out! I'm trapped!'

Her voice was very loud now, so piercing surely someone

would hear her even down here in the deepest part of the MTR?

'Help me! I'm locked in! Let me out! Unlock the gate!'

Her voice echo came back to her.

'Lock the gate!'

Then she let out a long, long swear word that hung in the air for what seemed an age. Then Candy stopped shouting. Her throat was sore and tight. Her mind was whirring with desperate thoughts. It was midnight. I'm alone. Anything could happen to me. Anything. How can I get in touch with anyone? The cell phone. I have to get the cell phone. It's the only way.

She scrambled back the way she had come and was back on the platform. The faces on the posters seemed to be watching her, laughing at her with their white teeth.

'Ha ha, Candy! Miss Stupid!'

'Oh shut up, you…you…phonies! You're not real! You're just pictures on a wall. I'm real.'

She tracked back to the right place on the platform, looked down and prepared to jump. But she didn't. The cell phone wasn't there. It had gone. She looked closer then moved up and down the track. It must be there. It must. This is the right platform. She checked. Yes, it was. The cell phone wasn't there. Something or someone had taken it.

'But that's impossible! It was there! Where are you?'

She howled another stream of rude words at the walls.

'Oh God, what do I do now?'

Candy's voice was a hopeless wail. Her whole world had been turned upside down. With a loud thump and a rattle she dropped her bag on the floor. She looked hopelessly around. There must be something.

Her eyes saw the silver metal grille set in the wall.

'In case of emergencies, press the red button and speak.'

The words on the sign by it were red.

Now she was at the machine, her hands either side of the grille, her eyes staring at the words. She pressed the button once, twice, three times. There was an electrical crackle and then the sound of breathing on the other end. There was someone there! Help was near!

'Hello. Hello. Is there anyone there? I'm trapped on the platform. Can you help me?'

But all she could hear was the sound of breathing, rasping into the machine somewhere and it wasn't her breathing.

'Can you help me? I know you're there. Please answer me. Please help me. I'm locked on the platform. Can you hear me? Help me, please. My mobile's gone. I can't get hold of anyone. Help me. Please.'

Her voice was getting louder and harder. Her lips brushed against the grille making her teeth tingle. Now she shouted at the breathing noise from beyond.

'Come on! Help me! Speak to me! Do something!'

The voice that came back slithered to her like a snake and grasped her throat, made the hairs stand out on her neck. She felt as if freezing cold water ran down her spine.

SHE FELT FREEZING COLD
WATER RUN DOWN HER SPINE.

'Candy's in trouble, isn't she? Deep, deep trouble.'

The voice hissed. The words spat into the microphone. Candy looked desperately around expecting someone to be standing there.

'Who are you? How do you know my name? You're supposed to help me. Get me out of here. Where are you?'

The voice rasped again like metal rubbing on metal.

'I'll get you out of there, Candy. Don't worry.'

Candy stared at the grille.

'You'd better do that,' she said trying to sound calm and in control. Her voice wavered and wobbled. 'Or you'll be in big trouble.'

The voice sniggered.

'Oh, I think the big trouble is all yours.'

Candy crashed her fist against the grille.

'Who the hell are you? Get me out of here…you…freak.'

Now the voice oozed a smile.

'Now don't go talking like that, Candy. Take it easy. You've cut your hand on the grille.'

She looked down at her hand. There was skin shaved from her knuckles and little beads of blood in a random pattern.

'How do you know that? Can you see me? Are you watching me? What's going on here? This is weird.'

She turned away from the grille, pressing her back against it to block the eyes that seemed to watch her through it.

'Okay, Candy. Time for me to come and get you. To help, of course. Just stay where you are.'

The voice was smiling again. Candy braced against the wall ready to spring away. Was this some sort of practical joke? A TV hoax show? She felt as if she were pinned to the wall, unable to move. She knew she had to get away before the freak found her. Get away. Anywhere. But where? Down the tunnel was dangerous — the electric line — one stumble, one touch and she was fried. But where else could she hide? She needed to hide, hide until tomorrow when the new day arrived and the trains began to run again. When everything would be normal again.

Candy went stiff with fear. The sound of footsteps echoed through the passageways and they were coming nearer towards this platform. She had to move but her feet seemed frozen to the ground.

'Hang on there, Candy!' His voice boomed in the chambers of the MTR.

It broke the spell that held Candy. She launched herself forwards. The rails rushed up to meet her and she landed on all fours like a dog between them. There was a smell of oil and metal. The stones between her fingers were greasy.

'No point in running, Candy. I'll find you. I'm much faster than you.'

The voice taunted her. She raised herself, pulled her bag tight onto her shoulder, looked straight into the dark tunnel ahead and ran.

She ran like she had never run before. She cut through the cold, still air, her feet pounding on the stones, splashing them onto the rails. It wasn't totally dark. There were signal lights still on, warning lights that bathed her in red as she passed. She could see ahead the track curved to the left. Maybe beyond that there would be somewhere to hide.

The blood was throbbing in her head and her breathing was heavy. The cold air burned in her lungs. The broken knuckle on her hand was sharp with pain. The wires and tubes along the walls seemed to snake past her as she ran. She seemed to have been running for an age — she must have left him — it — whatever — way behind.

Candy passed the curve and could now see the tunnel stretched straight ahead. She stopped and listened. For a moment — for a few hopeful moments — there was no sound. Perhaps he had gone into the wrong tunnel. Perhaps he couldn't follow her here. She strained her ears.

'Oh, I'm here alright, Candy. Just behind you. You don't lose me that easily.'

The voice only seemed to come from a few yards away. How could he travel so fast? So silently? She let out a cry then swore at him — a long stream of the foulest words she knew.

'Ha, Candy. Such language from a young girl. Tut tut.'

Candy launched herself forward again, pushing against the clammy air, hearing it roar in her ears, catching at the back of her throat. She plunged on, faster and faster.

Then she saw it, partly hidden between two brick pillars. A door — a service door. It had a number and another plastic plate.

Emergency Exit.

She raced to it, grabbed the handle and twisted. She stopped herself, stopped her desperation. She had to do this in silence. Her body pressed against the door and it swung easily on well-greased hinges. She was about to step through then paused, reached down, picked up one of the largest stones and flung it far down the tunnel ahead. It bounced and rattled off the rails somewhere in the darkness. Then she slid through the doorway and pressed it closed. She leaned her head against the door and listened for passing footsteps but there was nothing.

Behind her a steep flight of concrete steps disappeared upwards. They must lead outside to the real world, she thought. This is the emergency exit. Where else would they go? The real world where there were real people. Real people who didn't want to… .

'Ah ha, Candy. Hide and seek. My favourite game.'

The voice was hissing from farther down the track. He had followed where she had thrown the stone.

'But I'll find you. It's the blood, you see. The blood from your hand. From your little fist. I can smell it. I can smell it from here.'

Candy looked down at her hand. Blood was oozing from the cuts, sliding down her fingers, dripping slowly onto the ground. She had left a trail for him. She pulled her t-shirt sleeve down over the cut and clutched it in her hand.

The voice hissed again, nearer this time, just behind the

door.

'It's one of our special skills, you know. Finding blood. It's very exciting and very…necessary.'

What was he rambling on about? thought Candy. It didn't make sense. She turned and pushed upwards, up the concrete steps, two at a time landing her feet as quietly as possible. Her legs were pumping, the thigh muscles burning with the strain. Here was another landing and another flight of steps upwards. She flung herself forwards, stretching, pushing, stretching, pushing, up and away from whatever it was that was chasing her.

The door below crashed open like thunder. Was that his breathing she could hear? Feet were scratching concrete but so lightly, so quickly.

Candy surged on, her pulse pounding in her ears. Another landing. Another flight of steps. How many more? Then a door appeared. This could be it. The outside. Once there she would be safe. There would be other people. People to save her. To protect her. She threw herself at the door, wrenched at the handle and pulled. No movement. She tugged the handle down then up. No movement. She swore long and hard.

Then she saw the bolt that held it. Of course. To stop people getting in. She grabbed it and jerked it sideways. The door swung towards her and she was through.

It was an alley between two blocks of buildings, badly lit with rubbish strewn everywhere. Her foot caught against something soft that squealed and scuttled away into the darkness. For a moment she held onto the outer door handle. She looked down. A piece of metal piping lay in the gutter. A weapon? She turned to the door and hooked the piping through the handle and against the wall. That would slow him — it — whatever — perhaps enough for her to get away.

The alley led towards a narrow road where there was some street lighting. She ran to the end of the alley. The street was deserted. There were two parked vans and a lorry but no people. She glanced up at the buildings. They were all offices, stores — not where people lived.

The exit door in the alley rattled. She heard a muffled roar of anger from inside and the whole door frame shook. Even as she watched she saw the metal pipe bending as the door was pulled inwards. She gasped. What sort of man had that strength? This was no ordinary... .

Candy sprang off left, down the street past the parked vehicles. She'd gained a little bit of time. Behind her somewhere metal clanged. The door had been forced.

The street led towards a wider road. Surely there would be someone. A passing car? Someone going home late? There must be someone. The road opened up. There were more street lights. More parked cars. Some shops with the shutters up. But no sign of life. No lights in the windows. Nothing.

She had to move. Her legs felt like lead. Her lungs were

on fire. Her fist throbbed with pain. Why couldn't she think straight? There must be a way to escape. Think, girl. Think. He's quicker than you. You can't outrun him. You must hide. He will be in this road any second. Hide.

She ran past a row of cars flicking at the handles in the hope one would be unlocked. All secure. Another alley on the left. She swerved towards it. It was a dead end but half way down was a metal ladder dangling from the fire escape. The escape reached up the wall to the roof high above. At each floor was a platform. She grabbed the ladder with both hands and hauled herself up, hooking her feet onto the first rung. She pulled up straight and stepped up the rungs to the first platform. She threw herself onto the floor of the platform and pressed her body close, down as tight as she could. Her breath slowed. She had to be in control. She had to make herself invisible, silent.

Invisible, silent, she waited. Maybe he — that thing, that creature — had gone another way, had missed the alley.

'Candy! Candy! I think I hear you. I think I can smell your blood.'

The voice was coming from the road, bouncing down the alley up the ladder steps. Soon he would follow the words. How could he smell her blood?

Candy looked at her hand. The wound had opened as she ran and now blood dripped from her fingers which clutched the edge of the metal platform. She watched, mesmerised, as a tear of blood trickled onto the metal and then dropped earthwards. Could he hear it ticking on the ground below? She clutched her fist into her stomach but not before another tear of blood dropped.

Now there were steps in the alley. He was able to track her like an animal and on her ledge she cowered like an animal. He had stopped below her. She could feel him watching for her. In a moment he would begin climbing the ladder. But he was silent. Slowly she moved her head to the edge of the platform and peered down.

Candy could see only a dark-brimmed hat, wide shoulders — a man at least, tall and unmoving. He was looking down at his foot. Under his shoe a large grey rat was squirming, its nose glistening with blood.

'So Master Rat, it's your blood I smell is it? Foolish creature.'

There was a loud squeal of pain, a crunch of bone then a thin, hard laugh.

'Another time, Candy. Another time.'

Even as she watched he was gone, out of the alley, into the road — gone.

Candy began shaking. She was suddenly very cold. Was that it? Had she escaped him? Folding her arms into her armpits to stop the shuddering, Candy slowly got to her knees, then her feet, her eyes fixed on the entrance to the alley. Was he tricking her? No sound of footsteps. No hissing voice. Slowly, so slowly she lowered herself down the ladder.

On tip toe she moved through the slush and rubbish to the road. Carefully she edged her face round the edge of the wall.

The road was empty. She watched, watched and waited. The slightest movement she would see. But there was none. Now panic finally overwhelmed her and she began running up the road away from the alley, away from where he had been. Running as fast as she could. Running from the darkness to the light. There must be someone ahead. There was light. There was light!

'Candy, do you feel better now? Drink the tea.'

Her father's calm voice put its arm around her.

'She's had a fright. Look at you. Your hand. Let me clean it up.'

Her mother was there with a warm, damp cloth, kissing her cold forehead.

Father was kneeling in front of her and looking in her eyes.

'I won't ask what you were doing out so late. Not now.'

'She will tell us,' cut in Mother 'won't you?' Candy, when you're ready. Tomorrow. We're just happy that you're back safe, Candy.'

Candy's eyes began to fill with tears. She wanted to tell them everything. She wanted to tell them nothing. She wanted to sleep.

'Mom, I'm really tired.'

'Of course. Bed for you. Go, go.'

CANDY COULD SEE ONLY
A DARK, BRIMMED HAT, WIDE SHOULDERS - A MAN AT LEAST...

Candy hauled herself up. She felt giddy as she moved towards her room and hardly realised that the door bell had gone.

'I'll get it. Strange, someone knocking so late.'

In a daze, Candy fell face down on her bed, feeling sleep flooding in. Through the blanket of darkness she heard her father's voice.

'Candy! Someone has found your cell phone. Candy, there's a man here with your cell phone.'

Acknowledgements

My thanks go to Betty Wong, my editor and to Jan and Lucy, my reliable and trusty critical readers.